Praise for
A Wider Universe

"The characters who share the point of view in Allison Floyd's novel are appealing and recognizable, damaged and flawed. All are trying to make sense of a world of seemingly random misfortune and accidental luck. Sometimes by happenstance and sometimes with great effort, they gradually find meaning and even hints of grace. At the same time, the reader is drawn in by a deceptively simple story told with subtle insight, and finds meaning and beauty emerging where it was not at first apparent. *A Wider Universe* is a beautiful and promising debut."

– Bob Epstein, Associate Professor of English, Fairfield University, Fairfield, CT

"*A Wider Universe* certainly deserves wider attention. Allison Floyd's debut novel will keep your eyes glued to the page as you delve deeper into one family's drama and try to figure out what role faith plays in everyday life. It'll have you thinking about your own beliefs in fate, God, and religion as you watch a family come together in the wake of trage- dy after many years apart. It's a book that'll make you think of your family and the relationships you share with friends, neighbors, and newcomers. It's a wonderful, moving, and uplifting book that you won't want to put back on the shelf. You'll never want to go another day without talking to family when you're done with this story."

– Herb Scribner, author of *The Pen*

"Like Tolstoy once said, happy families are all alike, while every unhappy family is unhappy in its own way. With this story, Allison Floyd explores the intricacies of a family that must come apart be- fore it can come together. Each character taps into the raw emotions we've all felt at some point in our lives, making the story exceedingly relatable and enjoyable. Readers are guaranteed to find at least one character with whom they identify, thereby empowering them to immerse themselves in the narrative and invest in its outcome."

– Anna Papachristos, writer and author of the blog *Stop & Smell the Roses*

A Wider Universe

A Novel

ALLISON FLOYD

 Gere Publishing, Massachusetts

A Wider Universe
Allison Floyd

Copyright © 2016 Allison Floyd
Print First Edition ISBN: 9780974399591

Library of Congress Control Number: 2016954677
Publisher's Cataloging-in-Publication Data
Provided by Five Rainbows Cataloging Services

Names: Floyd, Allison.
Title: A wider universe : a novel / Allison Floyd.
Description: Shutesbury, MA : Gere Publishing, 2016.
Identifiers: LCCN 2016954677 | ISBN 978-0-9743995-9-1 (pbk.) | ISBN 978-0-9981987-0-5 (ebook)
Subjects: LCSH: Grief--Fiction. | Loneliness--Fiction. | Families--Fiction. | Spirituality--Fiction. | Self-actualization (Psychology)--Fiction. | BISAC: FICTION / Literary. | FICTION / Family Life.
Classification: LCC PS3606.L6865 W53 2016 (print) | LCC PS3606.L6865 (ebook) | DDC 813\.6--dc23.

Printed in the United States of America

"I do not feel obliged to believe that the same God who has endowed us with senses, reason, and intellect has intended us to forgo their use and by some other means to give us knowledge which we can attain by them."

– Galileo Galilei

Part I

1

✶ ✶ ✶

There was someone at the door.

The visitor had used the doorbell, which had been on the fritz for years, making not a typical bell sound, but rather a high-pitched buzzing. Anyone who frequented the house or had any familiarity knew to use the knocker, not the doorbell. Therefore, whoever was standing on Gene Shepherd's porch that cool afternoon in autumn was not someone he knew. It was a stranger. Gene Shepherd was weary of strangers and reluctant to leave his evening project. He sat alone at the kitchen table fiddling with the radio he was taking apart and slowly reassembling while halfheartedly listening to a rerun of M*A*S*H on the television. It was a Trapper John McIntyre episode of the classic sitcom, not a B.J. Hunnicutt epi-sode, which Gene preferred, but as he was only partially paying attention, it didn't make much difference. His aging Irish setter lab mix, Maudie, had curled herself around his boots beneath the table. When he heard the awkward high-pitched buzzing of his slowly, but dramatically dying doorbell, he considered ignoring it. He obviously did not know the caller, and frankly, was not very interested in company.

The bell buzzed again.

Gene made a mental note to start parking his truck in the garage when he came home from work. This caller obviously could tell he was home and avoiding answering the door. He returned his attention to the gutted radio on the table. Anyone with an ounce of brains would certainly give up and go away.

For a third time, he heard the buzz of the doorbell and finally decided to answer the door, even if it was to tell this person to get off his porch. He rose from the table and walked slowly through the hall from the kitchen, making no haste in reaching the door. The floorboards creaked beneath his boots with each slow but heavy step he took. At last he opened the door and found himself face to face with his decidedly unwelcome visitor. Before him stood a young man who looked to be in his early twenties. He had dark red hair and square-framed glasses, was tall and thin, and impeccably dressed in a collared white shirt and navy peacoat, complete with a bright red scarf around his neck. He had a smattering of freckles across his pale cheeks and nose and the Buddy Holly-esque glasses obscured startling bright green eyes. Although the youth was somewhat tall, Gene still towered over him from his more than six-foot frame. The young man was also holding a thick black-bound book at his side.

Here we go, thought Gene, *Jesus freaks*. This was not a visitor that he welcomed with open arms. He surveyed the young man, fresh-faced and young looking, awkward in his height and leanness. Gene doubted that the young man even needed to shave. He considered briefly closing the door in this kid's face, locking his door and returning to his kitchen. But before he could entertain this happy idea any further, his visitor spoke.

"Hello there, are you a resident of this household?"

Gene looked around, and then at the young man. This was a fairly bizarre question. *No*, he thought, *I just hang around in other people's houses hoping someone will come to the door*. Gene started to speak.

"This is my house, but I'm sorry, I'm not interested in buying anything; I don't like to sign any sort of petition and already know who I'm voting for, so…"

The young man cut him off.

"Sir, what I really want is just a few short minutes of your time." He smiled. It was a genuine smile that seemed alien on the face of anyone traveling door to door for a cause. It surprised Gene that he made his request with such innocent earnestness. He concluded that this kid was obviously still wet behind the ears. Gene said nothing. Truthfully, he had nothing to say. His mind had drawn a blank, and excuses for why this young man should leave his property temporarily eluded him. With neither a discouraging or interested acknowledgment of this young man's request, Gene simply raised his eyebrows. The young man took this as a green light to start his pitch.

"My name is Patrick Frye, and I'm from Utah, just outside Brigham City, a little town you've probably never heard of. I'm twenty-one years old, and I'm part of the Family of Jesus Youth Coalition. FJYC is a group of college-aged students, many of whom plan on becoming pastors or teachers in Christian schools, like myself. We're committed to spreading the word of Jesus. May I ask your name,

4

sir?" He said all this very fast and smoothly, as though he were reading from a perfectly memorized script. He reminded Gene of the way Technical Support addressed him when he called for help with getting a virus off of his computer: professional, with a poorly veiled and unsuccessful attempt at being personal.

Gene stared at Patrick Frye and then reluctantly said "Shepherd."

Patrick Frye seemed very pleased that Gene had agreed to play along.

"Well, Mr. Shepherd, it's a pleasure to meet you."

He thrust his hand forward, grabbing Gene's hand to shake without waiting for Gene to offer it to him. Enthusiasm seemed to be absolutely oozing out of the young man's pores; he gripped Gene's hand firmly and pumped it up and down several times.

"Sir, I'd like to share with you a little bit about what we do. We spread awareness of the Christian faith and educate others about the love of Jesus, Our Lord and Savior. Our missionaries travel to different countries to spread the word, we organize service trips to places in need of volunteer work and rebuilding, we're *especially* committed to rebuilding New Orleans, and overall, helping those who have lost their connection to Christianity find their way back." He grinned and looked at Gene expectantly.

Gene blinked, irritated with himself for entering into this uncomfortable exchange. He vaguely considered telling this kid he had the wrong house; that he was Jewish, or a Buddhist, or a member of a satanic cult, any little lie to get rid of his visitor. But he didn't. He wondered why he had even allowed the young man his audience for as long as he had. Gene was put off by preaching and people trying to impose their beliefs on others. Yet he was still standing on the porch staring down a youth who looked thoroughly convinced that he possessed the secret power and knowledge that could save even the blackest of souls. Gene highly doubted whether Patrick Frye from Utah had any clue as to what the man called Jesus, son of a carpenter, who lived two thousand years ago in a land that was now stricken with violent political conflict, was really all about.

Evidently Patrick needed no prompting, or even response from Gene before continuing.

"I'm currently a student at a Christian college out west; hardly anyone on the East Coast has heard of it, so I won't bother to mention the name. But I took the semester off to do some domestic missionary work. My job is to let *you* know what's going on." He reached into his black messenger bag, which looked sleek and expensive. He pulled out a red folder, and from it he removed what appeared to be several brightly colored glossy pamphlets.

"These," he said, positively bubbling over with ardor, "are verses from the New Testament. On each pamphlet is a different verse and how it applies to everyday secular situations. That way, even people who aren't very religious can incorporate Jesus into their everyday lives and see how his blessings directly relate to them. These handouts are short enough to read in just a few minutes. They are perfect for a quick daily reminder of the countless blessings of Our Lord."

He held his hand out, gripping three different pamphlets, extending his propaganda towards Gene who hesitated, then took them from the young man.

Patrick Frye seemed quite happy that he successfully transported his literature to another human being who clearly was not as religiously zealous as he was. Childlike triumph shone from his face and Gene was sure it was because the young man believed he had taken the first step in accomplishing his ultimate mission: saving souls, one Bible verse at a time. While Gene made no indication that he was remotely interested in what Patrick had to say, he also hadn't slammed the door in his face. He was sure Patrick considered this fact a victory in itself.

Patrick closed the folder and his bag, as his other hand tightened around his Bible.

"Well, Mr. Shepherd, I do appreciate you taking the time to speak with me, as I know Jesus appreciates you letting him into your life. I hope you have a wonderful day."

For the second time he grasped Gene's hand to shake, this time however Gene shook back, squeezing rather harder than necessary. He thought he saw the young man wince, almost imperceptibly, as his big hand tightened around the youth's skinny fingers. He watched as Patrick Frye turned on his heel and briskly walked down his porch steps, up the driveway, and back out onto the road.

A full minute passed before Gene moved. He wasn't sure what had just happened, or more importantly, why he had let it. He was not a man easily bothered or annoyed, but he also had no patience for the presumptuous nature of solicitors, particularly those of the religious variety. He felt there was something very cavalier about a person (*any* person, but particularly this irritating, smug kid) claiming to know what God or Jesus or Whoever wanted. Gene doubted very much that scrawny Patrick Frye had a direct phone line to the Big Guy.

He returned inside and stuffed the pamphlets into the trashcan in the kitchen. It's not like he needed Bible verses on hand. He knew there was a Bible somewhere in the house, maybe under the bed, maybe in the closet. He figured he would risk a smiting. They were, after all, only pamphlets.

He was washing dishes, scrubbing the pan from the casserole he had finished for dinner when Gene began to think about his strange visitor. *Where did this kid come from, outer space?* he wondered.

He was curious as to how Patrick Frye had found him, how he had decided to use the town of Foothills, Pennsylvania as the target for religious conversion. Lancaster County was a few hours south of Foothills, and Gene supposed Patrick might feel more at home with the Amish. The Amish community also might be a better target audience for a religious visitor like Patrick. Or perhaps Patrick figured he needn't bother with a community where the people were already so devoted to their faith.

Gene had seen many Amish people on his way to and from Philadelphia and frankly, found them less out of place than a "domestic missionary" knocking on his door. He recalled a summer when his daughter, Chelsea, was about ten. The Shepherd family was on its way to a summer house in Rehoboth Beach that they rented, when they pulled into a rest stop along the Jersey Turnpike. Getting out of the car, the Shepherds encountered dozens of members of the Amish community flooding the parking lot. Chelsea had been full of questions about "those people who look like they're in a play about the Mayflower."

Gene had explained to his daughter about the Amish and their lifestyle and clothing, and over the years the Shepherds saw their fair share of Amish people across the state. Philadelphia was also a place with a high population of Irish Roman Catholics, including almost all of Gene's in-laws, so he was not unfamiliar with religious communities. However, whereas the Amish and Irish Catholics were a part of Pennsylvanian culture, Patrick Frye stood out like a sore thumb.

Gene also wondered if it was a coincidence that the young man happened to prey upon a lonely widower. His wife, Marybeth Shepherd, had died December third, not quite a year ago, of ovarian cancer. Chelsea, now nineteen, moved out months earlier. Gene had been alone in the house, with the exception of the dog, for almost ten months.

Gene Shepherd was not the type of widower who intentionally avoided social interaction. He did not even prefer to be alone. But in the months since Marybeth died, he had not seen many people and did his best to keep busy, even if it meant working on a seemingly never-ending list of home improvement projects around the house. He still worked the same job he had for twenty-five years at the tractor repair and supply store as a mechanic and occasional salesperson, a job that required lots of customer interaction, and he was always friendly to just about everyone. However, he did not make friends easily. Marybeth informed him while they were dating that he suffered from a crippling case of social pacifism. He was either unable, or unwilling, to take the initiative in actively meeting new people.

His easy-going temperament did not stem from shyness, nor was it due to fear of confrontation or uncomfortable situations. He was simply a go-with-the-flow type of guy. He had friends, to be sure; in fact, you'd be hard pressed to find anyone in the town of Foothills who did not think highly of Gene Shepherd. He was very well liked and generally well known, especially since he had fixed around half the tractors in the county. He was simply not one to call up a friend to go to Sully's Bar for a drink or to invite his married friends over for dinner. He and Marybeth used to entertain reasonably often, and similarly were invited to other couples houses for dinner parties, but usually it was Marybeth who did the actual coordination of these get-togethers. Now, almost a year later, Gene still did not feel he was up to entertaining married friends when Marybeth's spot at the table was still so painfully and conspicuously empty.

Yet Gene was a smart man who knew all this time alone was not the healthiest environment for him. However, he was willing to give it a few more months of solitary mourning for his wife before reemerging into Foothills' social scene, if you could call it that. Marybeth had often teased Gene about his profound pacifism, saying aloud that she had no idea how he got anything done. She told him he was like an old river trudging along at his own pace.

"It's amazing you ever worked up the nerve to ask me out," she would often say.

Chelsea, who seemed to understand her father's disposition a bit better than her mother did, explained the situation to Marybeth one night over dinner.

"It's not that Dad is passive. He just doesn't give a shit."

Both Marybeth and Gene laughed in agreement, but Gene privately thought his daughter had only half explained the situation. To say that he did not care about anything was untrue. He was very principled, held fast to his solid morals, and was an unapologetic family man. The point he thought Chelsea was trying to make, was that he was very unmoved by what others outside his family and close friends thought or expected. Gene existed in a world where as long as he was living in a way that was right for himself and the well-being of his family, it didn't matter what others said about him.

Disregard for the judgmental eyes of others seemed to run in the Shepherd family; his own father, Emery, once painted a gigantic smiling chicken on the side of the family's barn on a whim when Gene was a child. This lighthearted act had annoyed Gene's mother and utterly embarrassed Gene and his brother, but Emery remained unfazed by their disapproval and the quizzical stares the painting drew from the neighbors. He loved that smiling chicken and he would keep it, naysayers be damned. Gene had inherited his father's indifference to peer approval, adopting Emery's philosophy of "live and let live" (although without his father's particular fondness for whimsy).

Perhaps this was one of the reasons Gene objected so strongly to visits from people like Patrick Frye. Listening to a stranger go on a religious rant made Gene feel as though he were having a physical reaction to a very unpleasant smell; he just couldn't stomach it. Gene was a firm believer in allowing people to conduct themselves how they pleased, without any outside pressure from others who were attempting to impose judgment or expectation upon them. As far as he was concerned, Patrick Frye and other religious solicitors violated what Gene believed to be his inalienable right to be left alone.

2

✳ ✳ ✳

For the second time in a week, Gene Shepherd heard the sound of his doorbell. For someone who so seldom had company on a regular basis, he certainly had a lot of visitors lately. Just in case it was a nosey neighbor paying a call, he stayed where he was, which was hunched underneath the sink, removing some troublesome rust from the water pipe, but he stopped briefly so he could hear the visitor. After a few moments of silence, Gene considered himself to be alone once again and resumed his battle with the rusty pipe. It had been a slow business day at work, and he had spent the majority of it behind the register instead of out in the garage, so when he got home, his hands were itching to fix something.

Gene found that there was almost always something that needed fixing. If nothing was in need of immediate repair, he knew there was always something that could use a good cleaning.

The doorbell rang again. Only this time it sounded more like the squawk of a bird stuck in a vice. The doorbell was nearing the final gasp of its life. Gene noticed Maudie giving him a reproachful look. Her hearing was not what it once was, but she was still irritated by the high-pitched nails-on-a-chalkboard whining of the bell. He reached over and scratched her ears.

"Who's my good girl?" he said, and she licked his hands affectionately.

Once again the sound of the doorbell filled the house.

This guy cannot be serious, he thought as he got up from the floor. Even if that insufferable little Pat Robertson-wannabe had not had enough nonsense the other day, Gene certainly had.

He made his way towards the door, wiping his dirty hands on the handkerchief that was hanging out of his back pocket. He opened the door hoping that by some miracle the person standing there was the UPS man bringing him a delivery and thus needing to use the doorbell so he could sign for a package. Not that he was expecting anything in the mail, nor did he know anyone who would send him anything out of the blue. Still, there was no harm in hoping.

But instead of a delivery person, the skinny awkward form of Patrick Frye stood in Gene's doorway.

"Uh, again?" he wondered aloud. It just slipped out.

"I beg your pardon?" asked the young man. He was still smiling expectantly, so Gene supposed he didn't hear what he had mumbled.

Gene wasn't often rude, and on the rare instance he was ever anything less than polite, it was because the situation warranted it. Still, at the moment he could not mask his surprise and annoyance that the young man had returned. In all the years Gene had lived in the house, he had been visited by maybe two other calls from religious solicitors, but Patrick Frye was back for the second time in less than a week. This was just strange. The kid had also spent several minutes ringing his doorbell and waiting, leaving him little choice but to answer the door whereas any other reasonable caller would have given up when no one answered his first ring.

Realizing he had been standing in silence for longer than was socially appropriate, Gene said, "I...didn't expect to see you again. I wasn't really expecting company today."

This hint was completely lost on Patrick.

"Well as it turns out I'll be in the area for quite a bit longer than I originally anticipated, so I thought I'd do a second round of the homes I've already visited. I need to wait for my transportation situation to work itself out before I can visit some of the homes on the other side of town and up in the hills."

Gene wanted very badly to say, "*thank you for sharing that*", but he kept his mouth shut. Some people were naturally chatty and liked to share a lot. Marybeth, for example, had always been very talkative and often shared things that Gene would not otherwise care to hear about or have any interest in, like the make and model of her hair dresser's new car or which of the high-end facial creams she had tried lately worked best for her and why. But she was his wife so he smiled and nodded. Patrick Frye was not a member of his family, a complete stranger and frankly, was bothering Gene, so he deserved no such consideration. However, Gene was never interested in confrontation, so he attempted to keep things on the polite side.

It also struck Gene as odd that Patrick mentioned he had already visited many of the houses in the area. This seemed rather unlikely, as the road Gene lived on, Hopikon Road, was quite a long walk from the center of the town, wound to and fro, up and down through the hills, and was at least four miles long before it turned into Quaker Street, which finally met with one of the main roads back to town. Without a car it would be an immense undertaking to visit all the houses along this part of town, and now Patrick claimed he was coming back for seconds.

"Well, why do you see the need for a 'second round'? Is there something you didn't tell me last time? You gave me those pamphlets, so I don't think you forgot anything."

"I feel like my approach was a bit too impersonal last time," explained Patrick, who looked troubled, as though he were disappointed in himself. "I spoke with my pastor since then, and we had a long talk about my approach to my missionary work. I realized if I used the same approach to everyone, it's not going to work, because everyone is different and coming from very different places. You have to be more personal with people to learn about them. Because in order for them to accept Jesus, you need to know about their lives…"

Gene cut him off.

"Yes, I'm sure it's true that you should be more personal with people who want to let Jesus into their lives, but for those of us who are all set, I don't think it's necessary to get more personal. I feel like I was pretty clear I'm not interested."

"Oh, before I forget, here are today's pamphlets. I thought you might like them," Patrick said, completely bypassing the bit about Gene not being interested. He went to reach into his side-bag for his folder.

"That's okay, I have a Bible!" Gene blurted lamely.

Patrick looked up, and then closed his bag.

Gene tried to backtrack. "What I mean is, I do own a copy of the Bible and I don't need pamphlets to explain to me how it relates to my daily life," he recovered. Not that he had ever sat down and read the book; he really had no reason to as it was old, and belonged to Marybeth, given to her at her confirmation. But Patrick didn't know that, so what did it matter?

"Well, Mr. Shepherd," Patrick continued, while Gene mused that the kid had remembered his name and wondered whether he should be alarmed, "maybe I need to use a more personal approach to convince people who think they are 'all set' to be more receptive to the idea of Christianity."

He looked at Gene pointedly, as though that settled *that*.

"I don't think that Christianity is essential in everyone's lives," Gene said. He didn't really want to get into the issue, and maybe if he could convince Patrick he was a lost cause, he'd give up.

Patrick, it transpired, was not the giving-up kind.

"It's the people who think like that who need people like me the most. They're the folks who have lost all connection to faith and live entirely secular lives, and so they don't go to church or bring their children up to believe. That's how atheism and agnosticism are spread."

Finally, Gene felt the need to speak up. If Patrick wasn't going to back down, then Gene wasn't going to let him get away with making judgments on non-religious people.

"I think you're failing to remember that religious freedom means we're all allowed to believe what we want, whether that's Judaism, Hinduism, paganism, or nothing at all if we choose. Actually, we have freedom *from* religion if that is our preference. I'm pretty sure there are even denominations of Christianity that don't insist you go to church or follow strict rules. They let you live your life according to your own conscience. I live by my own conscience, regardless of whether or not that makes me a good Christian."

The young man said nothing, waiting for Gene to continue.

"Just because I'm not a churchgoer doesn't mean I don't believe in anything. Faith to me is more personal than that. It's not about making a show of being in the pew every week. For me, it's about connecting with the world around us while we're here. It's not a set of rules and regulations you have to strictly adhere to. You don't have to fit into a perfect clone mold or you automatically go to hell. Who knows? Maybe heaven and hell don't exist."

"God is not an all-you-can-eat buffet, Mr. Shepherd," he said with a small smile as he shook his head. "A man cannot simply pick and choose that which he likes and discard that which he doesn't. It's hypocritical for someone to adopt the doctrines and beliefs that suit his lifestyle and ignore those that inconvenience him. He has to embrace it completely or not at all."

Gene paused. "You see things as very black and white, and what you don't realize is that there are many shades of gray in between. The world has changed and evolved in the centuries since your Bible was written. You can't expect everything in it to apply the same way in the world we live in today." He stopped. He sensed he was becoming too invested in the discussion.

"Anyway, I'm not going to wax philosophical with you because I really don't think what you're doing is right. I'm afraid I don't believe in proselytizing," he said.

The young man stared blankly. Apparently Gene had hit on a vocabulary word that Patrick did not know. The young man smiled uncertainly; perhaps he could get away with not knowing the word and only pretending to understand what Gene had said. It struck Gene as ironic, and somewhat obnoxious, that a self-proclaimed missionary wouldn't know what it meant to proselytize.

Gene Shepherd was feeling uncharacteristically antagonistic. Any other night he might have just told the young man in a kind tone thank you, he was not interested and if he visited again he would have to take legal action. But not tonight.

"Are you familiar with Sir Thomas More?" Gene asked.

"I have heard the name, but I'm afraid I cannot recall who he is," Patrick replied.

Like hell you've heard the name, thought Gene, *you're just pretending you're not as out-of-touch as you actually are*. He continued.

"He was an Englishman, a philosopher, you might say. I think he was also a lawyer. He wrote a book during the Tudor dynasty about a perfect society called *Utopia*. In this perfect society, there was complete religious freedom, much like we have here in America. Only in Utopia, it was illegal to try and convert others to your way of religious thinking. They weren't allowed to bother other people with their beliefs or try and persuade them that their way was *the* way."

Again Patrick gave no response, but he did lean up against the porch railing as though he intended to be there for a while. Making himself comfortable, he slung off his big black messenger bag onto the porch steps and placed his Bible on top of it.

Noticing this, Gene added pointedly, "I'm beginning to wish I lived in Utopia right about now, if you know what I mean."

"Mr. Shepherd, the only way to save people is for them to accept Jesus into their hearts as their personal savior. And for them to do that, someone has to show them the word, especially if they've been living purely secular lives. It's my responsibility as a member of my church and as a Christian to enlighten others, because if I sat back and did nothing, I'd be just as bad as an unbeliever. That's what we missionaries do. We help people see the Word and remember the Lord. That's why I'm here talking to you, to reacquaint you with Jesus. And it's not just folks in third world countries without access to a good Christian upbringing. People in our society are too distracted by the evils of modern science, television, and the internet."

It took a great deal of self-control for Gene to stifle a laugh.

"So what you're saying is I won't go to heaven because I watch television and don't have a close personal relationship with Christ?"

"The media does nothing but endorse sinful behavior like violence and adultery, and portray religious figures as naïve and obsolete," said the young man, whose face, Gene was surprised to see, was in complete and utter seriousness. "And everyone," he added, "should have a close personal relationship with Christ. It is the only way to salvation."

Gene took a moment to collect his thoughts.

As was his habit, Patrick Frye continued speaking without caring to notice whether or not his audience wanted to hear more.

"You'll find, Mr. Shepherd, that I am not your typical run-of-the-mill missionary. I *enjoy* engaging in conversation about my faith even with individuals who don't agree with my beliefs. I feel that it creates an opportunity for you to say your views, but also for you to hear mine. Every counter-argument you throw at me I believe I can refute. I am secure in my faith."

Oh good lord, Gene grimaced as he ran his hand through his salt and pepper hair distractedly.

"So nothing, not science, not logic, not philosophy or theodicy, or anything can even make you *question* the steadfastness of your beliefs?"

"I have complete confidence in my faith. I know in my heart and soul that this is what God wants."

...And there he goes again with his smug assuredness that he is divinely informed, Gene thought.

"I'm very glad for you," said Gene, his voice growing increasingly edgy. "It must be nice to know exactly what's going on in the universe."

Showing the first sign that he could actually perceive another human being's feelings, Patrick said, "Mr. Shepherd, I can tell this might not be the best time to continue this discussion. I'll plan on dropping by again soon."

Gene could not decide whether the young man was simply unrelentingly persistent or just plain stupid. Patrick Frye could plainly sense Gene's impatience and was picking up on his attitude by the tone in his voice, but he had just said something about dropping by again soon.

"It really won't be necessary for you to visit me again. As I said, Patrick, I'm not interested in individuals trying to proselytize on my property. I respect your right to believe what you want, but it's my right to believe what I want, and it's not your job to save my soul."

Patrick Frye surveyed Gene for a moment, looking mildly troubled. Gene could tell Patrick did indeed consider it his job, if not his divine personal mission to save as many souls as he could, starting with Gene's. Patrick quickly brushed the rejection away, and unfurrowing his brow, he smiled brightly and said, "Alright, Mr. Shepherd, you just have a nice day. God bless." He picked up his Bible, slung his bag over his shoulder, walked down the steps, and back up the walkway towards the road. Gene did not stop to watch him leave. Instead he went right inside and locked his door. Maudie sat at the foot of the stairs. When he bolted the lock, he saw her big brown eyes observing him quizzically.

"Don't look at me like that," he said.

3

★ ★ ★

Gene's next self-appointed task was to organize some of the clutter in the attic. He moved dusty cardboard boxes and plastic containers around and opened them, so he could identify what they contained, label them, and if necessary, discard or donate anything that did not need to be saved. He found some of Marybeth's old belongings, and packed them tight into a corner. *That* he wasn't quite ready for. He lifted the lid off another box that had the memorabilia Marybeth had saved from when Chelsea was little. The box was full almost to bursting with drawings, art projects, report cards, some favorite toys, and at the very bottom of the box, was Chelsea's very first pair of ballet slippers, faded, dirty, and very small.

Gene held one of the slippers in his large hand. It looked as though it were fitted for a doll. He examined it intently as memories of his daughter's childhood swept over him. From a very young age, Chelsea was always dancing. Just months after she started walking, she also started twirling, shuffling, swaying, and her personal favorite, bouncing up and down. Gene's daughter was in perpetual motion. Marybeth started calling her Mexican Jumping Bean, which was later shortened to just Bean, a nickname that stuck with Chelsea as she grew up.

The Mexican Jumping Bean's love of dance was insatiable. Gene frequently returned home from work to find Marybeth making dinner and laughing at Chelsea bopping around to the soundtrack from *Grease* or an old ABBA tape. When Chelsea was four years old, Marybeth bought her a pink tutu onto which she sewed silver sequins. Chelsea refused to take it off for a week. She insisted on wearing it every day to pre-school, over her pajamas when she slept, and would only surrender her glittery costume for bath time when Marybeth put her foot down on the matter. After a while Marybeth added a plastic tiara to Chelsea's ensemble. Chelsea told her parents that *now* she was a ballerina princess. Both Gene and Marybeth felt this indicated the need to put their very enthusiastic and energetic daughter into a dance class.

That was the beginning of Chelsea's foray into dancing. She began by taking a Tiny Tots dance class once a week, but loved it so much that she begged and pleaded with her parents to let her go more often.

By the time she was eight, it was clear that dance was not just a hobby, it was a talent. Chelsea was going to classes three times a week: tap, jazz, and ballet. She was still very young, but she took her art seriously. Her enthusiasm, mixed with some genuine talent and grace made her a standout from many of the other girls. She had a natural stage presence, and her vivacious personality only added to her appeal. For the entire month leading up to her spring recital, Chelsea could talk of nothing else but the fact that her teacher had chosen *her*, out of the whole class to dance a solo during one of the numbers, a jazz routine to "Take My Breath Away" from *Top Gun*. Marybeth rolled her eyes at this choice of music, but sewed glittery ribbons onto Chelsea's powder blue leotard none the less. At this time Marybeth was six months pregnant with their second child.

The Shepherds had recently found out they would were expecting a little boy, and they decided to name him Alexander. From the time Chelsea was three years old, Gene and Marybeth had been trying to conceive for a second time. Marybeth said she wanted her daughter to have siblings so that she knew what it was to share and always have someone to turn to, no matter what. Gene agreed.

After four years of trying with no luck, the pair was just about to look into IVF, which until then they couldn't afford, when they were thrilled to discover that Marybeth was again pregnant, and delighted to know they were having a son, a brother for Chelsea. With Chelsea it had also taken a few years of trying to get pregnant before Marybeth was able to conceive. The couple married the year after Marybeth graduated from college and passed her boards to become an RN, another three years until they decided to "pull the goalie" and start a family, but it was another three-and-a-half years before Chelsea was conceived, and by then Gene was thirty and Marybeth had just turned twenty-nine.

In preparation for the new arrival, the Shepherds painted the guest room a pastel baby blue and put Chelsea's old toys and Marybeth's favorite rocker next to the crib. Gene bought Marybeth a calendar, one with the pictures of dimpled babies in flower pots on it, to count down to June thirteenth, her due date.

On June eighth, Alexander David Shepherd came into the world stillborn at 3:44 in the morning. Marybeth was inconsolable and Gene was faced with the task of going home, where Marybeth's brother, Mitch, was watching Chelsea to tell her that her baby brother would not be coming home.

When he finally returned to the hospital, Gene was greeted with even more bad news. The doctor told the Shepherds that Marybeth should not have any more children, and that the probability of Marybeth even being able to conceive again was highly unlikely. There would be no more babies after Alexander. Chelsea was to be an only child.

The months that followed were the hardest that Gene and Marybeth experienced in their marriage until Marybeth's cancer diagnosis. For over a week after coming home from the hospital, Marybeth did not get out of bed. She kept the blinds closed and the lights off, and she slept for sixteen hours at a time. Gene was at a loss trying to explain to eight-year-old Chelsea when her mom would be back to normal. Privately, Gene worried if it was possible for his wife to return to normal, but all he could do was wait and see.

Marybeth eventually emerged from the bedroom and returned to her job as a nurse for the Visiting Nurses Association, during which she was able to present a façade of normalcy, but went through her daily routine at home like a zombie, halfway between denial and disbelief. Gene was unsure of how to help her. He wanted to support his wife in any way possible, but he was also dealing with his own grief while trying to keep up with Chelsea, who was as excitable as ever but seemed lost without a functioning mother.

Several weeks later, Gene was on his way back from a job repairing a long-time customer's tractor that took him almost an hour away from Foothills. It was a beautiful, bright sunny day and he was enjoying the drive, appreciating the winding, scenic route he was taking and the pastoral landscape whirring by. He passed a sign at the end of a dirt driveway leading to a farm that said "Puppies for Sale, Inquire Within." Instinct, more than anything, steered his Ford pick-up back around and down the dirt driveway. Only a few short minutes later, a heavy-set smiling lady took Gene behind her house to a pen where four Irish Setter lab mix puppies were tumbling around.

There were three male puppies and one female puppy. Their mother was an Irish Setter named Cleo belonging to the smiling lady. The pups' father was a rascally neighborhood chocolate lab. The owner explained that they were animal lovers but couldn't keep four more dogs. She said she wanted to make sure they went to good homes and seemed pleased when Gene told her he had a young daughter.

He and the owner exchanged some chitchat, giving Gene the opportunity to observe the puppies. While the brothers wrestled, chewed at each others' ears and yipped playfully, the female puppy remained quite content to sit on a bale of hay, occasionally trotting around the pen sniffing at the chicken-wire fencing curiously. The owner threw a worn tennis ball into the pen and the three brothers all chased it, one of them tumbling into the other two causing all three to wipe out. Their sister merely watched the ball pass then went back to her bale of hay.

A like-mind, thought Gene, and he asked the lady if he could hold the female puppy.

After five minutes of acquaintance with the pup, he knew she would make a good addition to the Shepherd family. She took to him immediately, and was quiet and calm. She seemed perfectly at ease, licking his neck and chin, which were in dire need of a shave. He paid the lady a hundred dollars, and she gave him the number of a good veterinarian and the names of the best dog food for puppies. Having nothing to transport his new pet in, the lady also provided him a large linen shopping bag, which the new puppy rode in quite happily all the way, resting on the passenger seat of the truck. That was how Maudie entered the Shepherd home.

Gene walked into the house toting the dog in the linen bag, and Chelsea, who was watching television and coloring absentmindedly, dropped her Magic Markers as Gene walked in the door. The bag her father was cradling rather than holding by the straps was moving, and from it she could hear faint whimpering sounds.

"Daddy, what is it?" she demanded, her curiosity bubbling over as she sprang to her feet and hurried to meet him in the foyer.

"Let's come back into the living room and see," Gene said.

When Gene lifted the dog onto the carpet, it was too late. Chelsea was in love. She immediately christened the puppy Maudie Fife. Gene was pretty sure she'd gotten the Fife part from reruns of *The Andy Griffith Show*, but he wasn't sure where "Maudie" came from.

"Why'd you pick 'Maudie', Bean?"

His precocious little girl rolled her eyes in an adolescent fashion and explained.

"Because, Dad," she said, giving a dramatic sigh far beyond her years, "That's her *name*."

Finally Marybeth came downstairs to find out what all the fuss was about.

Gene braced himself. He was not impulsive. He was deep thinking and a careful decision maker. To bring home a new dog without first talking to his wife was quite out of character. He hoped Chelsea's positively giddy response to Maudie might soften the blow of Marybeth's wrath for getting an unexpected pet—one that would need to be house trained, taken for walks, and cleaned up after, especially as a puppy. But instead of showing the slightest hint of anger, Marybeth got down on her knees and scooped up Maudie, hugging her to her chest. Maudie returned the embrace by covering Marybeth's face with doggy kisses.

Marybeth looked up at Gene and smiled. It was a sad smile, but it let him know he didn't have to worry about upsetting her; he could tell by the look in her eyes what her thoughts on the matter were: *you done good*.

In many ways Maudie Fife brought the family back together. Marybeth was more easily cheered up, Chelsea had a constant playmate who could keep up with her perpetual motion, and Gene had a calm, complacent companion for when he ran his errands, and when he sat on the porch at night for hours watching the skies. Maudie's favorite place to curl up was on top of Gene's boots, especially, and somewhat inconveniently, while he was still wearing them. The legs of most of his pants regularly ended up coated in an extra layer of brown Maudie hair each night. Gene did not mind. Maudie brought peace to his house, happiness to his wife and daughter, and warmth to his feet.

While the addition of a dog to the house was a good one, Marybeth still wanted her daughter to have some kind of childhood companion in lieu of a sibling.

"I would be lost without my brothers," she said one night as she joined Gene on the porch. "I want Chelsea to have someone she can always have, even after we're gone."

Gene suggested they consider adoption, which they both initially seemed very open to. They began to do research on the subject and contacted legal experts on the process, but after only a few weeks Marybeth confessed that her depression was coming back and she couldn't stand the disappointment if they were to get their hopes up and something were to fall through.

It was Tom, Marybeth's oldest brother, who came up with the idea. He had a daughter, Danielle, who was eighteen months older than Chelsea, and the two girls always got along very well during family gatherings. Tom lived just outside of Philadelphia with his wife, Sharon, and also had twin boys three years older than Danielle, Ciaran and Charlie. Tom's idea was to send Danielle up to

Marybeth and Gene's house one weekend a month and then have Chelsea stay a different weekend visiting Danielle with them.

"This way," he explained over the phone, "the girls can spend time together and Chelsea will have some sibling experience with Danielle and the boys. And it gives you two a whole weekend every month to yourselves."

It worked like a charm.

Chelsea and Danielle became inseparable, Chelsea got to spend quality time with her cousins during her weekend visits, and the Shepherds enjoyed having Danielle around once a month to help fill out their family.

This arrangement also gave Gene and Marybeth some private time to heal the romantic side of their marriage, which had taken an understandable hit after the loss of baby Alexander. After a few months of the new arrangement Gene and Marybeth were as happy as they could possibly be after having suffered the loss of their son.

∞

While Chelsea continued to pursue her interest in dance, taking several advanced classes through high school and joining her school dance team, her Mexican Jumping Bean excitement and perpetual motion changed into a calm serenity when she reached her teen years. By thirteen she had become a little quieter, and a little more self-disciplined. Although she was not the explosive ball of energy she used to be, she was still friendly and outgoing, but with a touch of rebelliousness Gene decided she had inherited from her mother, who was always on the stubborn side. While the Shepherds believed their daughter had a good head on her shoulders, they braced themselves for the moody and authority-resistant teenage years that their friends and family had warned them about.

Gene was by far the more laid-back parent. When Chelsea was sixteen and bleached her hair blonde and got her belly button pierced (without their permission, which was supposed to be required for those under eighteen) it was Marybeth, not Gene, who was upset. When Marybeth voiced her concern to Gene, he said that blonde hair and a ring in her belly wasn't hurting her, so there was no reason to be worried.

"At least she didn't get a tattoo," he pointed out.

Two months later, Chelsea colored the bottom layer of her hair back to brown but kept the top blonde.

"Sweetheart, you have such a pretty chestnut color to your hair. Peroxide blonde is not a hair color that occurs in nature," Marybeth told her when Chelsea got back from the salon.

Chelsea, who in her later teen years had matured into a temperament much more like her fathers, shrugged off her mother's criticism, and replied, "It's really not a big deal, Mom. It's just dye. It'll grow out eventually."

Marybeth said to Gene later that night before bed, "Since when did skunk become the latest fashion?"

Gene dared to rock the boat by pointing out jokingly that Marybeth had been coloring her hair blonde for the past few years.

"That's because I'm going gray, you dummy!" She gave him a playful *thwack!* on the shoulder with the paperback she had been reading. "Blonde dye covers up grays the best. Besides, that's completely different. I'm not being a teenager 'expressing myself' the same way a hundred other kids are."

Six weeks after Chelsea's new makeover, she met Greg. Greg Townsend had graduated high school two years before Chelsea, but did not go to college. Instead he worked for his uncle's construction company, mostly overseeing others doing the actual construction work. Gene Shepherd, ever the prize example of laid-back parenting, and the most accepting of fathers had at last met his match. This young man was not to his liking, not one bit.

Greg smoked cigarettes, had more than one ear piercing, and an air of cocky self-importance that Gene and Marybeth attempted, but failed to see beyond. Try as he might to accept his daughter's new boyfriend, be polite to the young man, or even smile, he always had a bad feeling about Greg. Of course, he never mentioned it to Chelsea. After all, he believed in a person making his or her own decisions, and knew that Daddy objecting to a boyfriend only makes the boyfriend that much more appealing. Besides, he was confident that Marybeth would do enough objecting for the both of them. She was not as guarded as Gene was about vocalizing her opinion. While she refrained from directly criticizing Greg to Chelsea, she made no secret that she was less than thrilled with the relationship.

Meeting Greg changed Chelsea's life dramatically, much more than she would care to admit or acknowledge. In Greg she found the exciting prospect of something new that could shake up her world. Chelsea had always been a good girl, always had her head on straight and her priorities in the right place. Greg, however, seemed to be the cliché that many girls are drawn to at some point in their lives, and Chelsea was proving to be no exception. Greg was a "bad boy" and though he really wasn't all that bad per say, Chelsea found his edginess intriguing. He was unlike the boys in her regular social group, and his smoking, drinking, and contempt for higher education struck Chelsea's curiosity. As someone who had always been on the right track herself, she found herself wondering what it was like to not always do what was expected of her.

At the start of their relationship, Chelsea saw Greg's lifestyle decisions as little more than typical adolescent rebellion handled in a James Dean *Rebel Without a Cause* fashion. As far as she was concerned, her parents' disapproval of her boyfriend was, in fact, a tragic misunderstanding. They were from a different generation. They did not understand. Plenty of young people did not go to college. Plenty of people her age drank, smoked, and made choices that were legally questionable.

Yes, Greg did on occasion experiment with drugs, but never enough to interfere with his work. Chelsea never found Greg's cocaine use to be a source of worry because he so seldom did it, and after all, part of growing up was experimenting and making mistakes. Chelsea was confident Greg would grow out of this phase.

After being together for over two years, she felt she knew Greg better than anyone, and she hoped, perhaps rather than believed, that he felt the same. Before they began living together, their relationship had been solid, and she accepted him for who he was despite some of his choices, banking on the hope that he would one day grow out of his reckless behavior.

At present, Chelsea was starting to worry that Greg *had* changed, and not for the better. Maybe Greg's behavior and lifestyle were turning more volatile, or maybe Chelsea was beginning to realize he was not growing out of this phase, maturing, and becoming more responsible as she once expected. He and his buddy, Adam, began using substances more frequently. What used to be an occasional indulgence was now an almost weekly routine. Chelsea herself had never tried cocaine. She was never interested, but as she didn't like to pass judgment on what others chose to do with their own bodies, she had no problem with Greg using it—so long as she was out of the house when he did.

Greg, for his part, was not used to following someone else's rules. With a functioning alcoholic father and a semi-disengaged mother, he had never needed to adhere to strict authority. He usually refrained from taking most substances in Chelsea's presence for almost the entirety of their relationship, with the exception of his cigarettes and beer, which he almost always kept on hand. However, lately he seemed to care less and less about when and where his drug use took place, and was no longer waiting until Chelsea left the apartment to do lines with Adam.

Chelsea knew she would eventually have to say something to Greg, and they would have to discuss what was and was not allowed in their apartment. Still, she was in no hurry to confront the issue, as Greg was becoming much moodier lately and the last thing Chelsea wanted was to start a fight.

4

Gene was upstairs changing a light bulb in the master bathroom when he heard the bone-chilling sound of his doorbell. He was certain Patrick Frye had returned for the third time in ten days, probably armed with holy water. He decided that this time he was going to hide until the young man left. His truck was in the garage so Patrick couldn't possibly know he was home, unless he was even more nuts than Gene thought, and had some sort of surveillance on him. Before he could linger too long on this creepy thought, he heard a much more welcome sound, the sound of a familiar voice.

"Uncle Gene, when are you planning to fix this doorbell?" Danielle had tried the bell twice, and after no response from her uncle, she sighed, pulled out her key and let herself in. She called out to him, sure that he was in the house. Gene had not been expecting Danielle. Her monthly visits stopped when she was sixteen, and though she visited frequently after that, it was usually to see her cousin. Since Chelsea had moved out, Gene wasn't expecting any unannounced visits from his niece, and was pleasantly surprised to find Danielle standing in his foyer.

Gene suspected Tom and Sharon may have encouraged Danielle to drop in on her uncle. But then, Danielle was the sort of thoughtful human being who didn't really need encouraging when it came to doing nice things for the people she cared about. Always an old soul and currently a junior at the University of Pennsylvania, Danielle was both mature and sensitive. She was also the type to drop all her college weekend plans, and drive two hours to go see her uncle who was lonely with only his dog to keep him company.

"Danielle, shouldn't you be at school?" Gene asked Danielle as she made her way up the stairs and dropped her duffle bag onto the guestroom bed that she always slept in during her visits.

"I have the rest of my life to get drunk every weekend, but not much interest in doing so," she returned, flopping down on the bed along with her bag.

"Well I'm sure you have a test to study for that you could get a head start on..." said Gene, in a false attempt to discourage her from staying. The truth was he was glad for the company, but did not necessarily want to appear too obvious about it to Danielle.

"Negative," she said getting back to her feet and looking around the room, "I took a huge microbiology test yesterday, so I'm free and clear from tests until midterms. Besides, I brought my MCAT study book with me which I'll probably go over after dinner while you're out with the dog."

Then before Gene could say anything, she marched downstairs and started rummaging in the kitchen to find something to make for dinner.

Over a meal of bacon cheeseburgers on toast (Gene had no hamburger buns in the house) Gene and Danielle discussed her plans for medical school, the Mets versus the Phillies (Danielle was a Phillies fan despite Gene's insistence that the Phillies and their fan base were pure evil—he was a loyal Mets fan in spite of the team's lack of consistency) and finally, the visits Gene had been getting from Patrick Frye.

Danielle was intrigued by her uncle's accounts of the young man. As a very bright collegiate young lady, she had a great deal to say about the self-proclaimed "domestic missionary" who had been dropping in on her uncle.

"I don't know what to say to the kid. Especially when it comes to trying to get him to leave." Gene said, finishing off the peas on his plate, "It's like trying to have a rational conversation with a crazy person. Or a donkey. He doesn't see reason the way normal people do, and he isn't even receptive to logical thinking. Everything he believes, in his mind, is the absolute truth."

"Of course it is," Danielle said, "that's what they're brought up learning. It's all he's been exposed to his whole life. We're lucky because we live so close to several different states along the East Coast. And big cities; we've got Philly, New York and D.C. within hours of us, so we get all the benefits of living in a cosmopolitan area. He's from out west in a very small town where all he's been subjected to is his religion. We have much more exposure to diversity and global issues."

"So you're saying he's been brainwashed by his secluded, western, small-town upbringing?"

"Maybe," she said in a noncommittal sort of way. "I mean, I kind of believe that most religions are a form of brainwashing anyway, but I'm not about to tell anyone what they can and can't believe...even if I think it's bull."

Gene smiled. Even if Danielle was not genetically related to him, she certainly shared some of his familial values.

Danielle shook her head and said, "I'm a biologist. I stick with what I can see in front of me. Philosophy of religion is an interesting field to theorize about, but no one can speak about spirituality with any kind of authority. Faith by definition cannot be proved or disproved so it's pretty difficult for someone to claim their religion is absolute truth and sound credible. Saying 'I believe this to be true' is one thing. Saying 'I know this is true and refuse to hear a word against it' is completely different. Because you can't. You can't *know*. " She leaned back from the table and pushed up the sleeves of her UPenn sweatshirt signifying that she was done with her meal.

Gene nodded and was silent for a moment.

"My biggest issue is his holier-than-thou attitude. He's got this maddening air of self-assuredness that he is divinely informed of The Truth," Gene said. "That kind of smug, condescending attitude drives me crazy. Honestly, it makes me want to slug him a little bit. That, and the fact that he keeps coming back."

"I say we stick this kid in a steel death cage with Tom Cruise, Harold Camping, and the Pope, and let them all duke it out to decide who really knows the truth," Danielle quipped.

After dinner Gene and Danielle went in separate directions. Gene had a few chores to do around the house, and Danielle watched some television before pouring over her MCAT book. When Gene finished fiddling with his DVD player, which had been making a whirring sound rather than playing his DVDs, he went into the living room and sat down in the easy chair. Danielle was sitting on the couch looking solemnly at her gigantic MCAT prep book, a pink highlighter poised aloft in her hand. It was the same spot in which Chelsea used to do her reading homework in high school.

He surveyed Danielle and thought about how different her life was from Chelsea's. Danielle was very smart, but she was also driven. She was currently majoring in biology, strictly on the pre-med track and had serious ambitions to be a doctor. She was particularly interested in pediatric surgery and working with premature babies in a neonatal unit, and also for some reason, she had recently shown a new curiosity in hematology.

Not only were Danielle's professional and academic priorities different than Chelsea's, so were her more superficial concerns, like her appearance. At the moment, she was wearing sweats and her light brown hair was twisted up into a messy bun, her reading glasses sitting at the end of her nose. Danielle was petite and pretty in a plain, understated way. She rarely wore noticeable makeup or flashy jewelry, preferring to keep her look comfortable and natural. Instead of looking as though she didn't care about her appearance, she simply looked nice in her own freckly fashion. She was also very no-nonsense and straightforward. With Danielle, everything was right there on the surface, she said what was on her mind, and often acted as if she had been a grown-up her entire life.

For a person who was so close to her cousin, she had very little in common with her. Danielle came across as self-confident and well-adjusted in both intellect and appearance. Chelsea seemed to Gene to still be searching. Chelsea was pretty in a sweet, round-faced, girl-next-door sort of way. However, she wore slightly more makeup than necessary, especially where eyeliner was concerned, always had French-tipped manicured acrylic nails, and dyed her hair a golden, albeit artificial, blonde color. Marybeth had told Gene she thought Chelsea lost herself a little during high school and was putting up a front so she would not have to deal with her emotional vulnerability.

"I think you're reaching, Dr. Freud," he had jokingly responded to Marybeth's psychological analysis. Gene actually agreed that his wife's theory might have some merit to it, but he also knew Chelsea was a teenage girl and it was not unusual for her to be searching. He also reasoned that and there were far worse ways than caking on the mascara for her to act out her adolescence.

Which she did, in due time.

Chelsea was not a troublemaker, and did not seem to feel the need to rebel much throughout most of her teen years. On the contrary, she was a good student, earned decent grades, and never stayed out past curfew. For a while she had talked about her ambitions to attend Penn State to study kinesiology, and maybe one day pursue physical therapy as a career. She had been excited as she looked through college catalogues and brochures, encouraged even more after hearing from an older friend that the dance team at Penn State was excellent. But somewhere between when she met Greg and when Marybeth was diagnosed with cancer, Chelsea decided that she no longer wanted to go to college, and stopped attending her dance classes. She graduated high school with a solid GPA, and no intention whatsoever of continuing on to further her education.

This had caused a significant conflict in the Shepherd house. With Marybeth struggling with the cancer treatments and Chelsea casting her future aside, there was just no pretending that their family wasn't in trouble anymore.

"I'm an adult," Chelsea had said calmly after announcing almost immediately following her high school graduation ceremony that she would be moving in with Greg, "This is my decision and I don't want to waste my time and your money going to college when I don't know what I want to do with the rest of my life."

Marybeth, so tired and weak from chemotherapy and being sick, her voice trembling in an effort to understand her daughter, said, "But college is a means of figuring out what's right for you. What happened to studying sports medicine? I thought you did have an idea of where you wanted to end up."

"I don't know if I'm even interested in that anymore," Chelsea said.

Marybeth tried an alternate approach.

"Why did you stop dancing, Chelsea? You love to dance. You've always loved dancing. It's like everything you cared about means nothing now with Greg in the picture."

Gene was at a loss for words. He knew he had no power to change his eighteen-year-old daughter's mind but wished he could, not only for the sake of his dying wife, but because he was certain they wouldn't be having this conversation if Chelsea had not been dating Greg. He had no issue with her perhaps taking a gap year to do some soul-searching, if that's what she really needed to do. But given her abrupt change in priorities and behavior, Gene was sure this was not coming from the real Chelsea. It was coming from the Greg-influenced Chelsea; a pod-like, watered-down version of his own child.

But Chelsea *was* an adult. Gene and Marybeth had no way to make her stay if she did not wish to live with them. His heart sank as he realized how far their daughter had drifted since meeting Greg; from her family, from herself. Suddenly everything she cared about, the life she had always known, was now very far away. The Chelsea that stood before Gene, decked out in her graduation gown, on a day that should be one for the photo albums, one of a parent's proudest moments, was not a Chelsea he knew. She was somehow a different daughter than the Mexican Jumping Bean who loved to dance and play, and cared about how her family felt.

And now it seemed Marybeth would never see that Chelsea again.

"I just..." Marybeth started, but her voice caught in her throat. She paused for moment to compose herself. Gene instinctively reached out and put his hand on her shoulder.

"I don't understand how someone who you have known for only a handful of months has changed your priorities so drastically. Chels, why are you throwing away your future for this boy?"

Chelsea had removed her cap and unzipped her gown, and very resolutely said "I need some time to figure out my life. I'm sorry. I can't do that here." She then retreated up to her room.

There had been distance between Chelsea and Gene ever since then, more so after Marybeth passed away. Gene turned his focus towards Marybeth, whose cancer had metastasized at a rapid pace. His wife refused to stop fighting the disease even after her doctors had given her a grim prognosis, electing to continue receiving any and all treatment she could, including a particularly punishing round of chemotherapy. When her doctors informed her that she was not responding to the traditional cancer treatment drugs, she tried homeopaths, integrative medicine doctors, Chinese medicine, anything that might help. Marybeth was fighting like hell to stay and Chelsea wanted nothing more than to go.

Gene did not know how to process the feeling of anger and betrayal he felt towards his only child for abandoning her mother when she needed her most, not for college which he had hoped, and could have easily understood, but to live with her boyfriend and wait tables. He believed a father loves his child no matter what, but he could not reconcile his bitter disappointment and resentment towards Chelsea. It was in the nature of a teenager to be shortsighted and self-centered. Yet somehow he wished his daughter might come to her senses in light of the fact that her mother was dying.

After Marybeth passed, Chelsea rarely stopped by the house. She felt like her father judged her for her life decisions and for her relationship with Greg. She gave him no chance to prove that no matter how bad he thought her relationship was, no matter how much he disliked Greg for being such an abysmal influence on his daughter, he still wanted a relationship with Chelsea. He hoped she would mature and realize what she had done, but it was tremulous hope since living with Greg was not exactly a shortcut on the express highway to Maturity Land.

Gene now looked up at Danielle, and ventured to trespass upon the Girl Network. He knew this was a risky undertaking as men were not usually privy to the Girl Network, by which information between female persons traveled at the speed of light.

"Have you talked to Chelsea recently?" he asked casually.

"Two or three weeks ago," Danielle said, not looking up from her reading. She made it no secret that she disapproved of her cousin's choices. Even though she and Chelsea had always been very close, Danielle found Chelsea's abrupt change in values and actions to be irresponsible and self-indulgent. Still, Danielle insisted on acting like an adult, even if Chelsea refused to do so, and continued to check in with her cousin every so often.

Before Gene could think of what it was exactly that he wanted to know about, Danielle spoke.

"Things seem to be going fine with her, she's working full time. I think she and Greg and a few friends were planning to go to New York City at some point but she was vague about when." Danielle was still pretending to read her book but it was obvious that she was eyeing her uncle beadily over her reading glasses.

Gene grunted in acknowledgment. He was glad his daughter was healthy and keeping out of trouble. That is, more trouble than being in a relationship with Greg had already brought her. Still, he felt conflicted about hearing that she was doing fine. A small part of him hoped that something would go terribly wrong and she would want to come home. He sat in silence.

Danielle suddenly spoke again.

"But I think there might be trouble in paradise."

It was all Gene could do to keep himself from jerking his head towards Danielle and springing up in his chair. Did she mean what he thought she meant?

"I mean, I wouldn't get your hopes up, Uncle Gene," she said, at last closing her book, marking the page. She took off her glasses to rub her eyes, looking tired and then put them back on. "But I get the feeling Greg is partying more than he used to and Chelsea's not happy about it. Like I said, don't expect her at the door any day soon but she might *finally* be picking up on how much of douchebag he is. So you never know."

This was not much, but it was a tiny ray of hope for Gene that his daughter was not completely in denial about her relationship. Eager to turn the focus away from Greg, Gene made a suggestion.

"Hey, I just fixed the DVD player and you've read that book enough for tonight. Would you like to watch a movie?"

Danielle demonstrated her interest by hurling her gigantic book across the living room.

5

✶ ✶ ✶

On Saturday morning Gene decided he should go to the grocery store and get some food for himself and Danielle to have for the rest of the weekend. He got up around 8:30, did a few odd jobs around the house, let Maudie outside, then got into his truck and drove to the store. He was gone less than an hour, and was in a fairly pleasant mood driving back to the house. He had saved some money on cold cuts and even decided to splurge on his favorite ice cream: pumpkin. Gene loved seasonal flavors, and the harvest season offered the tastiest goodies.

It was a beautiful autumn day, warm with a slight breeze, and the sun shined brightly. The leaves on the trees were no longer mostly green, and were gradually turning into yellows, oranges, and reds. He could smell fall in the air. Today would be the perfect day to get some work done in the yard.

He expected Danielle to still be sleeping. He figured that rising before noon was a completely alien notion to any college student. However, as he pulled into his driveway he saw that Danielle was sitting on the porch, her giant MCAT book on her lap, while Maudie trotted around the lawn investigating the many fallen acorns strewn across the yard.

As he neared the house, he noticed that Danielle was not alone on the porch.

He pulled up in front of the garage and could see clearly the familiar red scarf that Patrick Frye wore, even on such a warm day. He thought of going in the back door to avoid Patrick altogether. He was in such a good mood and the day was so perfect that he didn't want it spoiled by more talk of soul-saving, but he wondered if he might need to come to Danielle's rescue. Patrick had a special way of making a person feel cornered. Gene grabbed his grocery bags out of the bed of the pickup and wearily trudged toward his front porch, where he saw that his niece was having a spirited discussion with Patrick Frye.

Not wanting to interrupt their conversation just yet, Gene decided to hang back. Instead of heading right up to the porch, he stood listening a few yards away, partially hidden by the hedge.

"According to the timeline the Bible gives," Danielle was saying, "The earth was created only six millennia ago. But carbon-dating and a ton of other scientific evidence suggest the earth has been around for 4.6 billion years. How do you account for all the quiet time? What was God waiting around for?"

"The Bible is the word of God. God is infallible, and if the Bible says the earth was created six thousand years ago, then that is when it was created. I am no one to question these things."

"God didn't write the Bible, man did, and I'm sure they added their own editorial spin on its stories to suit their agendas. But that's another issue completely. You can't possibly take the Bible at face value about history and science; there is historical evidence of civilization in Egypt's predynastic period going back tens of thousands of years B.C.E. There's physical evidence that we've been around for longer than six thousand years. That's well before Christianity insists the earth was created," Danielle was crossing over from healthy debate voice into her *I go to college, therefore I am going to school you* voice. "Besides, *Genesis* puts

Creation about six thousand years ago, like you're maintaining, but God supposedly didn't make contact with Abraham until nearly two thousand years later. So God just sat around for a few centuries before breaking his silence?"

Patrick was becoming more disgruntled.

"Man may have done the actual writing, but it was God who dictated the Word through divine inspiration. The only agenda is to record the Word. And the Bible *is* historical. It mentions figures like Caesar and Xerxes and the Pharaoh Ramses, all of whom truly existed. It is a reliable historical text."

Gene chuckled quietly. Patrick seemed now to be grasping at straws. *Who was I kidding?* he thought. Danielle needed no rescuing. In fact, Gene would have bet big money she could actually make Patrick cry.

"I'm not saying there aren't historical things documented in the Bible; I'm just saying that scientific and historical evidence proves that it is not a reliable or even accurate account of the events and shouldn't be taken literally."

"Go ahead; check your 'historical' sources. Jesus Christ walked this earth, many sources have confirmed it. It's fact." Gene was surprised at how Patrick was getting sloppy in his arguments. His consternation over Danielle's refusal to concede any of his points was threatening the air of composed zealousness which was his hallmark. He now stood squarely on the defensive.

"Nobody's disputing the *existence* of Jesus of Nazareth;" Danielle shot back, "the question is whether or not he was *divine*."

"That," Patrick said stoically, at last trying to regain his composure, "is never a question."

"Of course it is! That's probably one of the biggest theological questions in existence," Danielle said pointedly. "It's perfectly reasonable to ask questions and speculate about philosophy and religion and the meaning of life. Do you actually think that your God gave you free will so that you could blindly follow Christian dogma unquestioningly?"

"You're right; God did give me free will. And with that free will I chose to follow not blindly but *absolutely*, because I know that is how one enters the kingdom of heaven. One can choose not to live by the God's word and without accepting Jesus, and although God still loves them, they cannot hope to be saved." Patrick's face had gone slightly pink, he was looking agitated, and Gene could see plainly that he was becoming very wound up. Patrick had undone a few buttons on his coat and removed his scarf as though the discussion were causing him to overheat.

"So you're saying anyone who's not Christian is going to hell, even if they are good people?"

"As I said, there is only one pathway to salvation and that is through Christ."

"Oh my God, you are seriously delusional. I bet you're probably one of those chuckleheads who thinks Jesus was a white guy, aren't you?

Gene took this opportunity to step forward from the rhododendron bush he had been haphazardly hiding behind.

He saw both Danielle and Patrick abruptly stop talking and turn towards him, both so absorbed in their debate they had not paid him any attention. Danielle looked to be thoroughly enjoying herself, her MCAT book now lying forgotten on the adjacent rocking chair. Patrick, on the other hand, looked as affronted as Gene had ever seen him. He supposed that the young man was more used to doors slamming in his face than young, precocious, future med students vehemently refuting his beliefs in rapid-fire dialogue.

"Mr. Shepherd!" he said looking relieved, something that amused Gene a great deal. "I've just been talking to your niece..." he tried to smile but he did not look very pleased.

"Yeah," said Danielle looking totally self-satisfied at having evidently rocked her young visitor's world. "He's been here for almost twenty minutes."

"I gave her some pamphlets—" Patrick began to say.

"And I gave them right back," Danielle interrupted.

"I thought she might find them useful," Patrick insisted, trying to regain some control over the situation. "It's very easy to fall off the path of God when you're of college age, constantly being tempted to abuse alcohol, experiment with drugs, and participate in promiscuous behavior and pre-marital sex."

He shot Danielle a superior look. Clearly he himself had not succumbed to such sinful temptations. When he turned back to Gene, Danielle crossed her eyes and made a face behind his back.

Gene was struck by how this young man never failed to stun him into stupefied silence. Patrick Frye was unbelievable, and he was back on Gene's porch, relieved to see him as though they were long-lost pals, and Gene had come to rescue him from the diatribes of an unbeliever like Danielle.

"I guess I didn't realize you would be back again, Patrick," said Gene setting down his grocery bags on the porch. "I was pretty sure that we talked about everything that needed to be talked about."

But Patrick was only half-listening. He was rummaging in his messenger bag and pulled out a Bible. It was a different Bible than the one he usually carried at his side. This one was not leather bound, but worn, somewhat dirty, and it had notes, bookmarks, and placeholders all over it.

"This," he said enthusiastically opening the book and running his finger down one of the pages, "is what I came to show you."

Gene looked down at Danielle who shrugged, but looked on intently.

"Last time I visited, you told me that proselytizing was wrong. I've come with proof that it is my mission to do just that in order to carry out God's work."

Two images flashed in Gene's mind in brief succession. The first was of himself, beating his own head against his garage door. The second was of Patrick Frye going directly from his house following their previous visit, straight to the town's public library and looking up the word *proselytize*. The first scenario seemed very appealing at the moment, but highly unrealistic. The second one seemed laughably realistic, and he had to quash the urge to laugh in Patrick Frye's lexicon-challenged face.

Feeling that he had not said nearly enough to this young man to get his disinterested point across, Gene followed Danielle's example and indulged him in a theological debate.

"Oh? And what is this proof?"

Patrick was almost glowing with pride and enthusiasm.

"*Matthew: 28*. Direct from the pages of the Bible," Patrick said, tapping the open page before him, and before Gene could stop him, he began reading aloud from the passage he had his finger on. The tone of voice in which the young man read the passage made Gene extremely uncomfortable, as though he was intruding on a love-sick teenage boy reading a sappy romantic poem to a girl. Patrick Frye looked as though he was performing an overly enthusiastic audition for a play.

"*Then Jesus came to them and said, 'All authority in heaven and on earth has been given to me. Therefore go and make disciples of all nations, baptizing them in the name of the Father and of the Son and of the Holy Spirit, and teaching them to obey everything I have commanded you.'*"

He closed the book ceremoniously as though he had just finished delivering his Sunday mass. Danielle mimed a particularly rude gesture behind his back. Gene had to chew on the inside of his cheek to keep from smirking.

"You see? Straight from The Word itself! This is exactly what Jesus wants. He wants people who have already accepted God's word to be responsible for shepherding others who are ignorant into the light."

Danielle snorted with poorly concealed but distinctly derisive laughter.

"You don't know the half of it," Gene said quietly to her.

But Patrick wasn't finished yet.

"I also did some pretty thorough research on Sir Thomas More," he said, extracting a spiral notebook from his bag and consulting what appeared to be some extensive notes. "He was martyred for standing up to dissenters of the church. Henry VIII had him silenced because he refused to stray from the true path. He might not have believed in missionary work, but he inspired other true believers to hold fast to their faith, which is just as important."

Gene's jaw dropped. While he attempted to compose himself, Danielle chimed in, "Henry VIII ordered his head hacked off because Thomas More refused to support his claim that his first marriage was invalid and wouldn't support his Act of Supremacy. Don't they teach you people history in school? Like *real* history, not 'And then Jonah was swallowed by a giant fish' mythological crap?"

Patrick dramatically shot her an offended look.

"Christianity is not *mythology*," said Patrick, as though the word left an unpleasant taste in his mouth. "We learn the history of man in school, but we know the history of God is paramount to understanding the history of man. You're too brain-washed by secular education to appreciate what an impact Christianity has had on civilization!" He was looking somewhat flushed again.

Danielle seemed to double over with glee.

"Did you hear that, Uncle Gene? *I'm* the one who's brainwashed." She half-laughed. She had a playful but biting edge to her voice.

Although Gene also appreciated the humor in the situation, he wanted to end the discussion, not prolong it. He said warningly, "Danielle…"

"I know, I know…I'm sorry," she said shaking her head with a knowing smile. "It's just like explaining quantum physics to a golden retriever."

"I know," Gene said, holding up a large hand to his niece and trying to elude Patrick, "I'm handling it."

Then to Patrick, who did not look pleased about being compared to a dog and was opening his mouth to rebut, Gene said, "Alright, so let's say for the sake of argument that this is your job, to convert others to your beliefs. Well, a car salesperson's job is to sell cars. That's fine. We all accept that. But not everyone wants to buy a car. You can only sell it to those who are inclined to buy in the first place. If a guy has no need or desire to buy a new car, then the salesperson is wasting time trying to sell it to him rather than an interested buyer. A lot of us don't want. Some of us were dragged onto the sales lot against our wills. Plenty of people have perfectly decent cars already."

Patrick Frye said nothing. Gene was already irritated that he needed to walk this kid through his argument, and Patrick was not making it any easier. For all the parables in the Bible that Patrick put so much stock in, he seemed to have trouble grasping the concept of a metaphor.

"What I'm saying is, you are the car salesman, and I am not interested in buying a new car. You should spend your time talking to people you have a better chance at saving. Or converting. Or whatever the hell it is you're doing. I'm sorry but I don't think you should come by here again. You seem like a nice enough young man, and I'd hate to have to call my policeman friend on you."

Patrick Frye merely smiled and said, "Very well, Mr. Shepherd. Danielle, it was nice to meet you." He grinned widely but his eyes looked terrified while addressing Danielle, who smiled and waved farewell enthusiastically.

Just when Gene thought he had at last won the battle, Patrick added brightly, yet somewhat ominously, "But God might drop me on your doorstep again someday." He turned and left.

Danielle rose from her chair and bent to grab her book and a few grocery bags. Gene followed her in the front door, whistling sharply for Maudie who lumbered up the steps and into the house. Gene shut the door and shook his head, exhaling loudly and making a point to deadbolt the lock behind him.

"What a nut," Danielle said as the door closed.

"He's a nut who doesn't know how to take a hint. Or recognize a blatant threat to call the cops."

"He's like a robot. He just kept repeating things like he'd been pre-programmed to think by the Bible Belt. He didn't seem to have any kind of normal human reactions."

Gene smiled.

"You mean apart from being terrified of you?" Gene headed towards the kitchen with his grocery bags.

"Yeah, that was kind of fun," said Danielle.

"How exactly did he stumble into *that* landmine?"

"Oh, before he headed over this way, I saw him put something in some of your neighbors' mailboxes. When he started up the steps here, and said he was looking for you, I asked what he was distributing. He showed me a bunch of little cards with a painting of Jesus' face on the front and something like *The Lord is my shepherd* on the back. I asked him if he was aware that it's illegal to put anything in a mailbox without a postage stamp."

"Stop," said Gene starting to laugh.

"He launched into some spiel about how spreading the word was worth risking a federal offense. That's when I put down my book and geared up for some fun."

"Unbelievable. Well hopefully he realized he was no match for you."

"Who knows?" Danielle said thoughtfully. Then she added, "But Uncle Gene, I really get the feeling he'll be back. 'Someday' might wind up being a lot sooner than you'd like."

6

★ ★ ★

For a small town, Foothills, Pennsylvania was very spread out. Houses stood separated from each other by patches of dense woodsy area, as well as by fields surrounded with fences and aging barns filled with tobacco. While neighbors often knew each other, it was not because of proximity. The further away from the center of town one ventured, the larger the gaps between the houses became. Up in the hills, it was common for there to be a football field's distance between a house and its closest neighbor.

Chelsea did not pay much attention to her neighbors. She and Greg lived in the upstairs apartment of a sizable three family house on Shays Street. She knew the residents of the other two apartments well enough to say hello and gripe about the landlord in passing, but that was the extent of their interaction. The adjacent lot to the right remained vacant for the time being, although the realtor's sign out front had said SOLD for quite some time.

The next house over on the left was a large yellow farmhouse which sat a few acres away with a grassy field separating the two houses. Chelsea had lived on Shays Street for months without ever seeing who lived there, and it was not until the mailman accidentally delivered an envelope to Chelsea and Greg's mailbox, 247B Shays Street that was actually meant for 235 Shays Street that her neighbor caught her attention. She looked at the address on the envelope, which looked suspiciously like a bill. It read: Alexander Jansson.

It was a warm Saturday morning, just past eleven and Greg was still sleeping off the beer and tequila shots from the previous night. Chelsea decided to walk the envelope next door and slip it in the mailbox. It was another few weeks before she actually saw what her neighbor looked like. She was on her way back from a run one day and she passed the man she assumed must be Alexander Jansson unloading groceries from his car. He did not look up or notice her pass by. He was tall, well above six feet, with a stocky build and broad shoulders. He had pale blonde hair and looked to be in his late forties, maybe even early fifties. Her curiosity satisfied, Chelsea thought no more about her neighbor.

Alexander Jansson had been a psychology professor at the University of Scranton for the past fifteen years, specializing in teaching behavioral and abnormal psychology. He was originally from Lund, Sweden and had grown up there. Before moving to Pennsylvania, Jansson taught at the University of Gothenburg in Sweden, where he had received his post-graduate degrees. He earned his undergraduate degree abroad at the University of Edinburgh. Having spent a summer session at Columbia University as an undergraduate as part of a study abroad program, Jansson was excited at the prospect of returning to the United States when he was offered a teaching position at the University of Scranton. A friend he had met at Columbia with whom he kept in touch and taught history at Villanova University had passed along the news of a job opening to Jansson. Jansson, feeling stagnant and restless at his current teaching job, felt that a change would do him good, albeit, a big change.

At the time, his wife, Margit, knew that he had applied for the job in Scranton, not believing that if offered a position the family would actually relocate to the United States. Whenever her husband talked about the position and the prospect of leaving Sweden, she laughed it off or rolled her eyes. She was sure this was just a bid to increase his salary at his current job by leveraging an international job offer and threatening to leave.

However, when Jansson announced that he had been offered the position in Scranton and he told Margit he really wanted to move there, she was shocked. Margit had no intention of leaving Gothenburg, let alone the country and certainly not the continent. She had never been to North America and had no interest in visiting, much less relocating there. She did not have a positive regard for the United States and frankly, did not care much for Americans. Not that Margit had actually met any Americans in her life. She based her distain and general dislike for the U.S population largely on media portrayal and political news stories.

Exactly a week after Jansson announced he had been offered a teaching position in Pennsylvania, Margit hired a lawyer and served Jansson with divorce papers.

As if the abruptness of his wife's actions were not enough of a shock to Jansson, before he knew what was happening, he had returned home from work one Thursday to discover that Margit had moved out of the house they shared (taking most of their shared belongings, such as the furniture, with her) and into a waterfront condo. She also had taken something much more valuable with her: their six-year-old son, Gustaf. A friend later informed Jansson that the owner of the condo was a co-worker of Margit's with whom she had been having an affair for the past year and a half, completely unbeknownst to her husband.

Were it not for his son, Jansson could easily have hired a good lawyer, dealt with the legalities concerning a divorce from Margit and left Sweden with relatively few complications. His discovery of his wife's callous betrayal and infidelity was enough to make him never want to see her again, and yet a little boy still connected them. He knew the courts would never grant him custody of Gustaf if he planned to leave the country. Margit was staying in Gothenburg, where the boy was born and had family, friends, and school, and no judge would separate a six-year-old from his mother and his home. Jansson then had an impossible choice before him: move to the United States and accept the job offer that had been the catalyst for the ruin of his marriage, or stay in Gothenburg and be with his son.

Gustaf was a shy, sensitive boy. He was very bright, and Jansson enjoyed reading with him. They spent hours together, Jansson reading aloud from thick tomes filled with epic adventures and

Nordic folklore. Gustaf sat mesmerized, completely enraptured by the tales. Jansson could not bear to think of his little boy being raised without him, and could not stand the idea of missing out on seeing his only child grow up.

That August, Alexander Jansson boarded a redeye to JFK airport in New York, taking with him everything he possessed, including a newly acquired gaping hole in his heart, and the image of a six-year-old boy's white-blonde hair, pale blue eyes, and freckly smiling face.

7

$\bigstar \, \bigstar \, \bigstar$

One of the calming pastimes in Gene Shepherd's life was stargazing. He had no scientific interest in the celestial bodies; rather he found a quiet connection to nature and the universe by sitting beneath the expansive sky on a clear night and staring at the vast space above him. He sat on his porch watching the sky for hours, finding it both comforting and intriguing. Raised in the Hudson Valley of New York, Gene was used to living far from distracting city lights and pollution, and was quite content to be able to view the infinite canvas of stars and planets from a rural setting like Foothills. His home was far enough away from any cities so that on a cloudless night, the vision of twinkling pin-pricks in the dark seemed to go on forever. He was glad. He had not always found such solace in gazing upon the heavens as he did now.

As he rocked in his chair, he could vividly remember being eleven or twelve years old, when a boy in his sixth-grade class, for no reason in particular and without being provoked, told him flatly one day at lunch that there was no God. The boy told Gene that his father was an atheist and so was he, and that there was no man in the sky with a beard pushing buttons and pulling levers so as to control the workings of the world. It was clear the boy had been given a talking-to by his father and he was merely parroting what he was told. But for young Gene Shepherd, this information, which had been given to him in such an abrupt and authoritative fashion, shook him significantly. This was not the sort of revelation he was prepared to process over tuna sandwiches and chocolate milk.

Even as a child, Gene possessed the capacity for calmness and composure to an almost superhuman extent. That afternoon he continued out the rest of the school day as though nothing were wrong. Neither his classmates nor his teacher had any idea that Gene Shepherd was anything but perfectly calm. Inside he was a wreck.

The Shepherd family went to church most Sundays, celebrated Christmas and Easter with the appropriate amount of reverence, and while his parents were not overly religious, they had instilled in him a belief system and moral values that had never been challenged until that point. This boy, whose name he could not recall decades later, (not that it really mattered) had planted a seed of doubt in his young developing mind. Although he was severely panicked internally, he returned home, told his mother his day was just fine, and marched straight up to his room. While he was bursting to discuss the matter with his mother, he refrained. He desperately needed her to reassure him that God existed and everything he knew about his faith and the church was true. He badly wanted his mother to tell him this boy at school was just being an instigator, but it was not in Gene's nature, even as a child to cause a disturbance unnecessarily. No doubt his parents would want to talk to his teacher, or worse, take up the issue with the other boy's parents which would be the worst of humiliations that his sixth-grade self could imagine. Instead, he waited for his brother, Carl, to get home from school.

When Gene was in sixth grade Carl was a senior in high school. Carl was somewhat of a loner and became increasingly separate from the family as he grew older. Surrounded by a world filled with Vietnam, Agent Orange, and the Watergate scandal and deeply mistrustful of others, Carl was not exactly the perfect candidate to ask about God when in need of an affirmation of faith, but Gene felt he had to ask *someone* and knew his teenage brother would keep the conversation private.

Eventually Gene heard his brother's heavy boots trudge up the stairs and the sound of his door shutting. Under normal circumstances Gene knew enough to avoid getting into any kind of weighty topic with Carl. However, considering how upset he was with the matter at hand, Gene decided to brave his brother's unpredictable temperament and knock on the door. Evidently, Carl was in a talking mood that day, and when Gene told him he had a question, Carl opened his long arms wide and said, "Ask me anything, little brother."

Gene explained to Carl what his classmate had said and asked him if he thought the boy was telling the truth. Carl thought about it for a moment, and then said, "Well, it kind of makes sense, doesn't it?"

Then he was off talking a mile a minute about conspiracies, wars, crusades, police brutality, conflicting religious ideology and several other points that refuted the idea of God, none of which made much sense to an eleven-year-old Gene. After fifteen minutes of respectfully listening to Carl, Gene told his brother, thank you very much, that he had answered his question and then proceeded to shut himself in his bedroom once again. In an effort to put all thought of religion out of his mind, he picked up one of the *Hardy Boys* books and began to read. By the time his mother called him for dinner, his thoughts were no longer focused on his crisis of faith, and had turned to chicken fried steak and the chocolate cream pie he knew his mother had prepared.

However, after supper Gene went outside where his father was boarding up a hole in the fence through which various critters had been getting into the garden. He happened to look up at the sky. It was a clear night and he felt he could see every star in the Milky Way. His father talked to him absently as he worked about the difference between diesel fuel and regular gasoline and how they worked in an internal combustion engine, Gene was straining his eyes to see any hints of heavenly objects. Heaven was supposedly in the sky, and that was where God, the angels, and his grandmother were supposed to be.

He offered up a silent but urgent prayer.

Please, give me some hint, some sign that You're up there!

He had no sooner finished this desperate plea when a small voice inside his head, one that sounded very much like the boy at school's voice, said "But there's nobody up there, remember?" With this thought he felt as though the bottom of his stomach had dropped out from beneath him and a gripping fear took hold of his heart. He searched the sky, desperate to see some trace of something spiritual, anything that would prove that little voice wrong, but all he saw were gaseous balls of light billions of miles into space. He had never felt more alone in his life. No God in the sky not only meant that everything he had ever been told about religion had been a fallacy, but it also meant that everything he knew, everything around him was meaningless, empty and without a greater purpose.

He quickly told his dad that he thought he had some math problems to do for homework and rushed inside the house.

Over thirty-five years later, Gene still remembered the lonely, sleepless night that followed his desperate prayer. He wanted never again to feel that gnawing sensation of uncertainty in his stomach, so he resolved himself to not think about religion at all. When he sat next to his mother at church when the family attended, he would not listen, instead he would go over times tables in his head, or count the number of ladies wearing hats in the pews.

As he grew into adolescence Gene was able to recover some semblance of faith, and eventually developed his own beliefs. He read about world religions in school and also did some additional reading on his own out of curiosity. He and Marybeth used to have long, deep conversations about faith and the universe when they first started dating (having been raised Catholic, she brought an entirely new viewpoint to the table.) Secure in the knowledge that he could never *really* know, Gene did not dwell upon the existence of the divine or worry about something that he did not have the power to change. His feelings about God were based more on his gut feeling, his own personal belief, separate from any religious denomination and ideology.

Now, as he leaned back and looked at the sky, he did not see it as empty and godless, proof that only science explained everything. He saw the night sky as an affirmation that not everything could or should be explained, and felt that the beauty and serenity of the universe was only further evidence of the awesomeness that God, or the Clockmaker, or whatever omnipresent energy had created it.

Sitting on his porch with Maudie around his feet was almost a nightly ritual. It was a time of quiet and reflection, as well as a constant reminder to appreciate the world around him. When he and Marybeth were newly married she would often try to sit with him on the porch, chatting happily about her day at work, the vacations she wanted to take, news her brother had told her about her young nephews. Gene liked to hear his wife talk. He took comfort in her constant chatting, but found himself drifting away while looking at the stars. Marybeth quickly learned that his time on the porch was Alone Time, and she started saving her chats for dinnertime and pillow talk. When Chelsea was a baby, Marybeth would set her on his lap and return inside. This way he could enjoy his quiet reflection and still be able to spend time with his daughter, who was too young to talk and disturb his stargazing. Incidentally, it also allowed Marybeth at least an hour of time to herself to take a bubble bath or watch a TV show without having to worry about the baby.

Gene reached down and scratched Maudie's ears absently. Tonight, for some reason, he was channeling his eleven-year-old self, and the sense of aloneness he had felt. Only this time, it was not God who was absent. It was Marybeth. It was Chelsea. It was his brother Carl, and his parents. Try as he might, he could not pretend that waking up alone, going to sleep alone, eating meals and passing long hours alone had not brought him any sadness. Maudie's constant presence was of course, a comfort, but it was not the same as having another person to talk to, to see, to connect with, and this conscious knowledge of the unhealthiness of being alone weighed heavily on his mind.

He knew he was lonely. He felt Marybeth's absence profoundly, but he missed his daughter even more, his only child, who at this very moment was most likely with her good-for-nothing boyfriend, preferring a life with Greg rather than a connection with her family.

After Danielle returned to school, Gene had no visitors for several weeks. He finally he called up his married friends Hank and Sally Cartwright and invited them to dinner. They very happily accepted the invitation and brought an apple pie for dessert. Gene cooked lamb chops and potatoes au gratin, something he had learned from Marybeth, and the three had a pleasant evening together.

The Cartwright's had two children still in high school, and they told Gene about how their eldest, Dylan, was a junior, and so he was busy looking into different colleges. Gene regretted asking about the kids. He liked the Cartwright children, but hearing about how they had college ambitions while he had no idea about his own daughter's life, upset him.

After his company left, Gene quickly felt alone once again. However, he was glad he had plucked up the courage to call and ask them over. He liked the feeling that he was able to have visitors again; good company, very unlike a certain bespectacled Bible-toting young man.

8

★ ★ ★

Gene Shepherd was born in Rhinebeck, New York. When he was ten, the family moved to Boyertown, Pennsylvania where Gene's father had inherited a larger farm from an uncle. Gene was used to living in a rural environment. He had few friends, but they were good friends, whom he remained close to even after high school and to the present time.

He attended college at Syracuse University where he met and became fast friends with Tom McClory. In the dorms they lived on the same hall and had two classes together. Gene's easy going nature was a perfect foil to Tom's infectious friendliness and irresistible charisma. Tom was also from Pennsylvania, just outside of Philadelphia and wanted to be a corporate lawyer. Gene was interested in business and economics.

One weekend Tom's sister came to visit. She was a senior in high school who was preparing to attend the nursing program at Drexel University the following September. When Gene and Marybeth McClory were introduced, there was immediate interest on both sides. Gene, ever the predictable social pacifist, was not one to speak up about his attraction to his friend's little sister.

Finally, after weeks of Gene trying to casually ask him about his sister, Tom said, "Just call her already. Here's the number."

Gene called the very next day. He went to visit Tom over the summer, and he and Marybeth started dating while he was in Philadelphia. They saw each other every few weeks and over vacations, and it was clear to both of them that they were very serious about one another.

Gene never finished college. A few weeks into the first semester of his junior year, his father had a massive stroke. Emery Shepherd lost the use of the entire left side of his body, and was unable to continue to run the farm. Gene immediately packed up his belongs and moved home to Boyertown to take over for his father. It was difficult to see his dad, who had always been so energetic and enthusiastic about nearly everything, struggling to speak and be understood, unable to walk, needing help eating, bathing and moving around. It broke both Gene's heart as well as his mother's, to see the sadness in Emery's eyes as he sat in his easy chair, unable to do anything but watch Gene tend to the land that he had worked so hard to make prosper.

To make matters worse, Gene's brother, Carl, had disappeared several years earlier. The year after Gene's crisis of faith, Carl had been drafted to serve in Vietnam. Despite his official request to be classified as a conscientious objector, he wound up serving several months in Southeast Asia. Carl was said by almost everyone to be "not quite right" after his tour of Vietnam. Privately, the Shepherds and those closest to the family felt that Carl had never been "quite right" by normal standards. He was moody and introverted, but highly opinionated and prone to erratic behavior. While Emery and Helen Shepherd knew their oldest son was considered odd, they didn't do much about it when he was growing up, as there wasn't much they could do. It was just the way their son was wired. They carried on raising the two boys as if Carl did not have any issues.

After Carl returned from the war, it was impossible to ignore that there was something very wrong with him. He would go days without talking, and then lose his temper and fly into a rage at the smallest provocation. The rest of the family would come home to the house looking like a disaster zone, furniture overturned and the contents of all the kitchen cabinets littering the countertops and table, even spilling onto the floor and Carl would be sitting stonily in front of the television as though nothing were wrong. One day Gene returned home from school to find that Carl had painted all the windows black while Helen was out running errands. A few times he had duct-taped the mailbox shut, which made for a very uncomfortable conversation for Emery with the mailman explaining his son's "situation."

As best Gene could tell at the time, his brother did not sleep at night. He frequently heard Carl banging around in his room at all hours doing who knows what, or sitting alone at the kitchen table in the pitch dark. Gene would return home from school to find Carl asleep on the couch. He seemed to only want to sleep in daytime, and sometimes jerked awake looking shaken if Gene passed through the room even though he was careful not to make any noise at all.

After a year of this, Carl simply took off. One summer night he'd packed a knapsack and left before sunrise, leaving a hastily scribbled note to family saying:

I can't take it, I had to leave. Don't look for me, and don't worry. I know how to survive.

Gene was fifteen at the time, and couldn't understand how his brother could simply disappear. His parents tried to locate Carl for weeks, but had no luck. After a while they began to carry on as usual, as though Gene were their only son. Gene suspected that it was too painful for either of his parents to even talk about Carl, so they pretended there was no Carl. The only evidence of another Shepherd son was a large family photo taken when Carl was ten and Gene was four that sat prominently on the mantel in the living room.

Gene wondered what would happen should Carl ever turn up. The family certainly had a case to have him committed to some kind of psychiatric hospital, but he knew his parents could never have their son institutionalized.

Over the next few years, the Shepherds heard from Carl only a handful of times. They received a dozen or so postcards, each from a different city, each one postmarked further out west than the previous one, not giving any detail about where he was working, or even if he was working. Still, it was proof that he was alive. Every few months the phone would ring, and there would be no answer from the person on the other end of line. Emery

Shepherd said he was sure these calls came from Carl even though Carl never said anything.

After Emery's stroke, the burden of his personal care and maintaining the farm fell on Helen and Gene. Gene worked the farm from sunup, to sundown, and Helen, who worked part-time at the local public library, had to come home from her job and work outside with Gene. Though she would have liked to stay home and care for her husband, she could not afford to quit even a part-time job, so she had to hire an aide. She later admitted to Gene she needed to borrow money from her sister's husband, who was quite wealthy, to pay for the aide. Gene couldn't imagine how hard it must have been for his mother to have to ask her brother-in-law for a loan.

They had no way to contact Carl to tell him about the stroke. This both saddened and frustrated Gene. He thought his brother should know about their father's condition, and that Emery Shepherd deserved to see his oldest son again, even if it was just once more before he died.

Gene also had no clear understanding of Carl's erratic behavior. What is now easily identifiable as Post Traumatic Stress Disorder was then an enigma to Gene as a teenager and to society, often cast off as "shell shock." He knew deep down Carl had always been strange, and that he must have seen and done things in Vietnam that were damaging to his mind and soul. That didn't stop Gene from harboring a deep resentment towards his brother who was lost somewhere out west, wandering as he pleased while Gene woke up at dawn every morning to keep the farm going and the family afloat. Carl was also not around to witness the effects of Emery's stroke as Helen and Gene were. He remained totally unaware while his mother and brother could only sit back and watch as Emery slowly deteriorated.

One day, Gene happened to pick up the phone during one of Carl's phantom phone calls.

"Hello?"

There was no answer.

"Hello...?"

Still nothing, though Gene thought he could hear breathing.

"Carl!" Gene's heart was hammering for reasons he could not explain. "Carl, don't hang up!"

He heard a sharp intake of breath.

"I don't care if you talk or not, just listen. Dad's sick. He had a stroke a few months ago." Gene paused to listen. He could still hear wheezing. The caller had not hung up...yet.

"He wants to see you. He needs to see you. You should come back. Dad deserves to see you one more time before—"

Click.

The call was disconnected. Carl had hung up.

Gene continued seeing Marybeth while he lived with his parents. Being in Boyertown he was much closer to Drexel University than he was in Syracuse, so they were able to see each other more frequently. Marybeth was very fond of Emery Shepherd, and he was of her, and she liked to sit with him while Gene was working. Emery was unable to speak with much clarity after his stroke, so he listened as Marybeth talked to him. She did not mind. Chatting came easily to her, and she was raised with the belief that family was the most important part of life, so she was eager to be close with Gene's family.

One weekend over the summer when Marybeth was visiting, Gene was outside doing some yard work. While Helen Shepherd was out shopping, Marybeth sat with Emery and talked to him. Although Emery couldn't respond to her, he sat and placidly listened while Marybeth chatted about her family and what she was learning in nursing school.

Gene was around the back of the barn doing repairs on the tractor, so he was not in the house when the doorbell rang. As Emery couldn't walk without help, it was Marybeth who went to the door. She did not recognize the man standing before her and was not about to let a stranger into the Shepherd's house. The man was tall, carrying a knapsack and looked scruffy and unkempt. He seemed uneasy, and eyed Marybeth with suspicion.

"Can I help you?" Marybeth asked.

The man was silent for a moment.

"I'm Carl," he said at last.

Marybeth was taken aback. Gene had of course told her about his brother, but she knew no one had seen him in years. She wasn't sure quite what to do or say, but she was spared having to make any decisions as Carl swiftly brushed past her and through the door before she had any time to think.

She turned and followed him into the house. She had heard about how Carl was unpredictable and not quite right, and she considered running to find Gene, but she did not think she wanted to leave Emery alone in the house with him. When she reached the kitchen, she saw Carl standing across from where Emery was sitting at the table.

The two men simply looked at one another. Carl said nothing and Emery could not speak, so they merely locked gazes. Marybeth saw Emery's eyes squint in recognition. Whatever spark of energy he had left flickered in his eyes at seeing his son, yet his physical condition kept him frozen in his chair.

Carl looked alarmed, almost frightened. He was standing several feet from his father and was leaning somewhat far back, as though Emery had some sort of infectious disease that Carl might catch if he got too close.

Marybeth stood cautiously across the room, feeling uneasy. She looked from Carl to Emery and back again wondering what would happen next. She surveyed Carl. On closer inspection, she could see how he looked like Gene, tall, with light brown hair, hazel eyes, with a strong chin and a steady glaze. Carl was leaner than Gene and had more severe facial features, but beneath his dirt and scruff she could see the distinct resemblance between the brothers. Only Carl was dirty and looked underfed, his arms were all sharp angles where Gene's were sturdy and strong from physical labor. Carl also looked older, much older than he should for his age. He was only six years older than Gene and still a young man, but something about his face and eyes told her he had aged in a way that others couldn't and didn't want to understand.

The kitchen was silent. After several moments that seemed to last an eternity, Carl opened his mouth.

"Dad," was all that he said. It was not a question or an exclamation, merely a statement.

Emery narrowed his eyes again and made a noise like he was clearing his throat. With a tremendous effort, Emery appeared to be trying to stand up, to no avail.

Carl took a tiny step forward and then jerked back again. Another moment later and he had turned and walked briskly out of the room, through the front door and away from the house. Marybeth and Emery were alone once again. She went up to Emery and squeezed his shoulder, saying softly, "I'll be right back, okay?"

She went out the back door to find Gene and tell him what had happened.

9

✶ ✶ ✶

The days were growing colder. September had come and gone and now October seemed to be passing quickly. The leaves on the trees, which only days ago had been brilliant shades of orange, red, and yellow, were now turning brown and falling from the branches at an impressive rate. Gene had overslept. He had a lot of chores to do around the house and yard before the weather changed and snow season arrived. He intended to spend the whole weekend outside working from dawn until dark so everything would be finished before it got to be too cold.

However, he couldn't bring himself to wake up early after having gotten back late from Philadelphia the previous night after attending a Phillies-Mets game. Gene was excited to see his team play, but they had lost spectacularly to the Phillies in the last few innings. Despite watching the Mets lose, Gene relished the chance to get out and spend time with friends. He was invited by his friend Ron, a Foothills police officer who had three sons between the ages of nine and fourteen, but only one spare ticket, so rather than choosing between his bickering kids, he offered it to Gene.

Gene first met Ron the day Chelsea was born. When he came home from work for his lunch break, Marybeth, in the middle of making lunch, went into labor. Cool as a cucumber, Gene picked up his wife's already packed suitcase, turned off the stove, and called her parents and brothers telling them the baby was coming. He then helped the very pregnant Marybeth into her Volvo (there was no way he was getting her into his truck) and backed out of the driveway.

A few short minutes into the drive Marybeth's labor seemed to have sped up with a vengeance, contractions coming at increasingly shorter intervals. Growing anxious, Gene stepped on the gas pedal. It wasn't until he saw flashing lights behind him that he realized he had been doing almost seventy miles an hour in a forty zone.

The cop that pulled them over was Officer Ron Sciaruto, and when Gene rolled down his window to offer up his license and registration, the officer could see Marybeth in the passenger's seat, huffing and puffing and shrilly gasping in loud bursts "Are you kidding me?! Are you kidding me?! We're getting a ticket *now*?"

Instead of writing Gene a ticket, Officer Ron Sciaruto got back into his cruiser, turned on his flashing lights, and escorted the Shepherds to the hospital. Two hours later, Chelsea was born. Gene and Ron had been friends ever since.

So when Ron called offering Gene not only a night to get out of the house but a chance to see a baseball game, he jumped at it. Ron was in the middle of a divorce and was also in need of a good, old-fashioned guys' night out as much as Gene was, complete with beer and fried food at the stadium. It had been a good night, but Gene hated oversleeping when there were chores to be done. In the end it didn't matter much that he overslept. Before he could head outside he realized he needed to clean out his toaster which didn't seem to want to toast the English muffin he had hastily shoved into the slot because it was so full of crumbs. He made short work the project and was glad to be able to move on to the next item on his to-do list: cleaning out the gutters before he could begin raking and bagging the leaves that were starting to blanket his entire lawn.

He put on a very warm, bright red plaid flannel jacket, buttoned it up as high as it would go, and went outside. He felt his breath catch in his throat. The air was much chillier than it had been all week, and the wind brought a hint of bitter cold suggesting that winter was well on its way. Despite the cold temperature, Gene was happy to be outside.

At least the sun is out, he thought.

Gene loved everything about his house and the land it sat upon. He felt connected to his little piece of earth; his rural sanctuary. He loved the view of the changing leaves and their beautiful colors along Hopikon Road. One day when Danielle was still making her monthly visits, she and Chelsea had looked up *Hopikon* on the internet and found that it was the Lenape Indian word for "shoulder." Gene felt this was a perfectly appropriate name for a road that wound between the hills.

Gene retrieved his almost brand-new and still shiny ladder from the garage, and set it against the left side of the house. He would start at the corner and work his way across the gutter to the right side of the porch roof. It was bright and clear day, but the wind was frigid and punishing. Gene was inspired by the chilly breeze to work more quickly in order to keep warm. He was hard at work, utterly absorbed in his task for a good forty-five minutes before he heard something that was more bone-chilling than the brisk autumn temperature.

"Hello! Mr. Shepherd!"

The young man's voice had yelled his name to get his attention. Between the wind and the scraping noise Gene was making by cleaning the gutters, it was difficult to hear. Even though he was still facing his house, his back to the street, Gene knew exactly who was standing in his yard. Patrick Frye had struck again. Gene continued to focus on the gutters under the pretense that he had not heard his name being called.

"Hello there! Mr. Shepherd!"

Patrick Frye certainly had persistence down to an art.

Gene stopped what he was doing. He turned his head in the direction of his visitor. There was Patrick, peering up at him through his glasses. His red scarf was wrapped particularly tight around his neck, and he was wearing a heavier winter jacket instead of his navy peacoat.

"I apologize," the young man called up the ladder, "but I recently had a long visit with your neighbor, Mrs. List, and what she told me explains a great deal as to why you aren't as receptive to Jesus as you could be."

That was it. Gene threw down his tool with a slam, not really caring that it came down very close to where Patrick was standing. He lumbered down the ladder, stomping slowly and deliberately as he hit each rung. When he reached the ground, he stared down Patrick Frye with a menacing look Patrick had never seen before. In fact, Gene had only made such a face two or three other times in his entire life.

Diane List lived across the street and two doors down in a little dark blue house. When Chelsea was little Diane's daughter, Michelle, used to babysit for the Shepherds. Every so often, if Michelle couldn't sit for Chelsea, Diane would volunteer to watch her for a few hours. Marybeth would frequently go over to pick up Chelsea at the end of the night and wound up staying for over an hour while Mrs. List prattled on and on until Marybeth had to make up an excuse to leave. She was a nice enough lady, but she was overly chatty and could be a terrible gossip. It wasn't until Mrs. List told her some pretty private details about another neighbor's life that Marybeth realized she should refrained from sharing anything personal with her. What had this woman told Patrick about him?

"What is Diane List telling a complete stranger about me, Patrick? And what business does she have discussing anything about me with you?"

For the first time since Patrick had gone head-to-head in a theology debate with Danielle, he looked worried. Remarkably, he seemed to shake it off, and even managed a bright smile.

"Please don't be angry with your neighbor, Mr. Shepherd. God wants you to love your neighbors. I was visiting her, and I mentioned I'd been to see you a few times and that you didn't seem all that open to the subject of God and being saved."

If Gene Shepherd had been a dog, he would have growled then. It was the only action that accurately expressed his state of mind. He felt as though his head were actually on fire. Instead of growling, he made no noise; he simply glowered at the young man. He couldn't speak. There were absolutely no words that conveyed the appropriate amount of anger and frustration he was feeling.

As he tended to do, Patrick continued speaking without waiting for Gene to say anything.

"Mrs. List and I had a good long talk about your hardships, sir. I now feel like I can grasp why you've been so resistant. Losing a child, losing your wife to cancer, and then your daughter moving in with a delinquent must be extremely trying on your faith. She also told me about your vagrant brother, the Vietnam veteran who disappeared and how your dad suffered a stroke at such a young age. All these things are tragic, absolute heartbreaks. But they are challenges sent by the Lord. God would not give us these trials if he didn't think we could handle them. They exist to make us stronger and test our faith. It's our job to overcome them and show Him our faith is unshakable."

Gene opened his mouth to stop Patrick from carrying on like the incredible ass that he was, talking about Gene's family like he knew them, and acting like he had the right to comment on his life, but all that came out was a small noise like a snarl. Oblivious as ever, Patrick did not even notice Gene quietly combusting right before his eyes. He kept right on talking in an upbeat, cheerful voice that made this intrusion feel even worse because he truly had no idea how far over the line he had gone.

"I now understand that someone who has suffered these losses might shy away from Jesus. But many people misunderstand these challenges. They think God is punishing them, that He is unjust. This isn't true. Just look at Job and all he suffered. Look at Abraham, and Isaac, and all those who suffered for their faith. Look at Jesus, who died on the cross. There is no reason to be angry at God because of these tragedies. God is what helps us get through our hardships. But there's still time for you, Mr. Shepherd. You still have a chance. I can help you, if you'd like." He finished with a smile, innocent and earnest and utterly infuriating.

If it were possible for a human brain to implode, Gene's might have done so at that very moment. This was too much. Most people would have slammed the door in Patrick Frye's face the very first time he appeared at their home. Gene had allowed him an audience on more than one occasion and then politely declined solicitation each time. He had been more than patient with this kid and was always civil, but this had officially gone from bothersome to harassment. The situation was turning creepy; now the young man had started to collect information about him, personal details about his life and family, and was coming back to use his deepest hurts against him as a reason to find religion. Why had this little freak chosen to fixate on him? Plenty of people dismissed religious solicitors, and plenty of people dismissed religion. This was the United States. Gene was allowed to be unreceptive to someone else's religion and have his own beliefs. He owed this young man nothing. Patrick Frye had no right or expectation that Gene Shepherd would be open to discuss anything, religious or otherwise, with him.

Not to mention Diane List. How could anyone be so insensitive and prying? Who was she to offer Gene's life up on a platter as an example of someone who shuns faith, when she was not even particularly religious herself? What had he ever done to deserve his personal life and intimate details about his loved ones being put on display for a stranger on a personal crusade, a twenty-one-year-old no less, who refused to leave him in peace?

As though emerging from a mental fog, Gene suddenly registered that Patrick had mentioned losing a child. Mrs. List must have told him about baby Alexander. It was bad enough she had clearly given him details about Chelsea, but to talk about Alexander was unforgivable. He also knew in his bones that Marybeth would never have spoken to Diane List about Carl. His father's stroke may have come up in conversation but Gene knew his wife, and she would not have discussed his transient and damaged brother with anyone outside of the family and close friends. How in the hell could this woman possibly have gotten this private information about him?

For the first time in his conscious memory, Gene felt like he wanted to hit someone. He had never struck another human being in anger, but found he very much wanted to hit the young man standing on his lawn. He clenched his fist and dug his fingernails into his palm to quell the urge to take a swing at Patrick. He took a few deep breaths.

At last, he found his voice. It was not the voice of the Gene Shepherd that anyone had ever met. It was not the calm, collected man who was known for his superhuman pacifism. This was the voice of an angry man.

"How *dare* you presume to pass judgment on me? How dare you go prying into my life? You don't know anything about me. You march up to my door, force your way into my personal business, and then you think you have to right to come here and keep trying to force your religion on me? I told you before, you're not welcome here. You have no business talking to my neighbors about my wife, or my brother. Who the hell do you think you are? You have some nerve showing up here again and talking about my kid!" He wasn't sure whether he meant Chelsea or Alexander, but discussion of either one of his children was completely out of line so it didn't really matter.

At this point, Gene was actually seeing red. His peripheral vision seemed to decrease as he saw the red scarf, while staring at the maddeningly ignorant individual before him. He was so furious, he could have thrown something. It was lucky for Patrick that Gene had nothing on hand to throw. Gene had grown up on a farm and was strong as an ox. If he threw something and it hit you, you were not getting back up in a hurry.

Patrick, for his part, had lost his smile and gone pale very quickly. This was not at all the reaction he had expected from a man whom he'd only ever see be civil and reasonable.

"Mr. Shepherd," he said trying to regain control of the situation, "I don't— "

But Gene cut him off. He'd had enough.

"Do not speak to me like we're friends. Do not address me like we know each other," he was shouting now, his voice booming. "In fact, don't speak to me at all. Get the hell off my property, and never bother me again. And if you ever discuss me or my family with anyone after this, you'll be praying to your savior that you never left Utah."

Patrick Frye seemed to be utterly frozen in place. There was true fear in his eyes, but he looked as though he were unable to move or speak. Finally it was dawning on him that Gene Shepherd, who towered over him at an inch over six feet with his solid build and giant hands, presented an actual physical threat.

"*Get out of here!*" Gene hollered and at last Patrick started to back away slowly. He then picked up his pace and broke into a jog in order to put as much distance between himself and Gene Shepherd, who for the first time in his life had reached his boiling point.

Part II

10

★ ★ ★

Chelsea Shepherd glanced up at the clock on the wall. It was just past four in the afternoon. The lunch rush at the Mountain Range Grille was long over, and it would still be a while before customers started trickling in for dinner. Since she was between tables, she decided to get some side work done. She was rolling silverware, happy for a few minutes off her feet, and she took advantage of the temporary slow business to sit and think undisturbed. She felt uneasy. Normally she was very good at leaving her personal problems at home, but today she couldn't shake off how frustrated and confused she felt about the state of her relationship with Greg. She sighed, brushing a stray lock of blonde hair away from her face, and wished things could go back to how they used to be with Greg. Lately they had been so out of sync.

The first time Greg came into her life, Chelsea had just finished dance team rehearsal at the high school. It was a Friday afternoon in April of her junior year, and her friend Brianna, who was also on the dance team, invited Chelsea to join her and a few other girls at her older brother Jacob's apartment. Even though she was tired and felt the very early signs of a cold coming on, Chelsea agreed to go to Brianna's brother's place, where they planned to order pizza and hang out, free from anyone's parents.

By the time the two girls arrived, already at least a dozen people had gathered. Chelsea sat and talked with a group of her friends and introduced herself to some of Jacob's friends. Jacob and three other guys sat at the kitchen table playing some kind of drinking game with a deck of cards, cracking open new cans of beer every few minutes. Chelsea happened to look up as the guys jeered at the loser of the hand, and noticed one of them looking at her.

She went back to talking, but could still feel his eyes on her. She knew that look. It was a look that many young girls are familiar with once they reach adolescence. She knew she was being checked out, but she wished he would look away. She could not give him an appraising look in return with his eyes glued to her.

After over an hour of pretending she wasn't looking at him, Brianna pulled Chelsea into the bathroom and said, "You know that guy, Greg, at the table with my brother? The one with the tattoo?"

"Yeah sure, I saw him," said Chelsea.

"He keeps asking about you." Brianna grinned at Chelsea, expecting Chelsea to bubble with excitement. "He asked me if you have a boyfriend and he thinks you're cute."

"I would hope so; he's been staring at me all night."

"So go talk to him! He's pretty hot. Did you see the size of his biceps?"

Chelsea had not noticed any biceps, as he had been sitting in such a way that they were not on display, but she was suddenly very curious. She told Brianna that if he was interested he could come over and talk to her. Less than ten minutes later he had sauntered over to Chelsea who was pretending to be deeply interested in a story her friend Kristen was telling, and said, "So why haven't you come and talked to me yet? You've been watching me this whole time."

He had a big grin, and he sounded cocky, but in a friendly way. He also smelled good, like a woodsy cologne. He had big brown eyes and shortly cropped dark hair.

She also saw that Brianna was right—he *did* have impressive, sculpted arms, one of which was encircled with a tattoo at the bicep. Chelsea couldn't tell if it was tribal or Celtic or Nordic but it definitely added to his physical appeal. Tattoos were sexy in moderation, especially if they had a special meaning behind them and weren't just ink for the sake of ink, something generic like an eagle or a girl's name. She made a mental note to ask him what it meant at some point.

"I think you've got that a little backwards," she told him. "I'm pretty sure you've been watching *me*."

"Well what can I say; when I catch the eye of the prettiest girl in the room, I might as well make an effort to talk to her. And since we're talking now, I'd say my watching you has paid off nicely. I'm Greg." He held out is hand and she shook it. When their hands touched Chelsea felt a warm sensation shoot from her fingertips, up her arm and down to her stomach where she was definitely feeling butterflies.

They talked for almost an hour. He was two years older than her, and had graduated from high school in the next town over. As they talked, Chelsea hardly noticed anything or anyone else at the party until her friend, Kristen, asked her for a ride because her parents were calling her every five minutes and insisting she get home immediately. Before she left, Greg made sure to get her number. By the time she pulled into her own driveway, she found that she already had a text from him asking her out. The two went out for burgers that weekend. From then on, they were inseparable.

Chelsea only had one boyfriend before Greg. His name was Max, and he was perfectly nice, perfectly smart, and perfectly good-looking; everything a first boyfriend should be. He was tall, blonde, athletic, and had been a big track star at the Foothills high school. They dated during Max's senior year. Chelsea went with him to his prom, attended his graduation, but the two decided to go their separate ways when he left for college at the end of the summer. He was attending Colgate University and neither thought that a long-distance relationship between a college freshman and a girl still in high school would work out very well. The split was amicable and the two remained friends.

Greg was a different story altogether. While Max had given her the pleasant sensation of butterflies fluttering in her stomach, Greg made every atom in Chelsea's body buzz. There was an immense physical attraction between the two of them, which only intensified their emotional connection. While they were able to have long conversations that were deep and meaningful, they also couldn't keep their hands off each other. During the first few weeks they were dating, Greg told her he liked her dancer's body, especially her legs, and that her flexibility was a turn-on because it meant she would be limber enough to "do things". This kind of talk was new and intriguing to Chelsea. When Greg would softly say something like this in her ear she would get goose bumps up and down her spine and felt her face flush hotly. She and Max had done their fair share of fooling around and Chelsea had enjoyed it, but her relationship with Greg awakened a physical curiosity in her that had not been there with the handful of other boys she had kissed.

Just over a month after they started dating, the two had sex for the first time in his bed. He was the first person Chelsea had ever slept with, and they continued to have a very active physical connection throughout their relationship. Even when they disagreed or were in a fight, they still seemed to keep their sex life strong.

Both Chelsea and Greg enjoyed living an active, fun-filled lifestyle. They would rather go out than stay in, preferred to go for a hike or a bike ride than see a movie. They often would take weekend trips together and were very much driven by the prospect of excitement. In a way, they were good together because it seemed neither of them wanted to stand still for very long. Chelsea loved Greg's spontaneity, always wondering what their next adventure might be.

Now, after almost two-and-a-half years together, something seemed to be off. They were planning fewer exciting activities, Greg became less inclined to do anything terribly active, and the two practically never went on real dates. Greg was partying more regularly, drinking several beers during and after dinner, even on nights when it was just the two of them. Also, much to Chelsea's displeasure, he was using cocaine with greater frequency. While his sexual appetite did not dwindle, he often initiated intimacy when he was very drunk. Chelsea disliked doing anything physical when Greg was sloppy and under the influence, so she had taken to making herself scarce when she knew he would be drinking or partying, electing instead to go to a friend's house or volunteering to cover someone's closing shift at Mountain Range Grille. This meant that a key aspect of their relationship, the great sex, happened far less often.

Chelsea wondered why her boyfriend was suddenly drinking and doing coke all the time. As far as she could tell, nothing had really changed in the past few months that would lead her to believe that he needed more excitement in his life or that he was unhappy in any way and needed a recreational outlet.

Truth be told, Greg had a reasonably easy life. He was extremely well-connected within the community, which he used to his advantage. He had a nice cushy job as a supervisor at a major construction company owned by his wealthy uncle. His uncle overlooked Greg's shortcomings and didn't penalize him for showing up late to the jobsite because he was hung over. He had previously done actual construction work for the company, but moved up quickly to a less physically demanding, better paying management position, mostly due to nepotism rather than meriting a promotion based on hard work and job performance. Greg also paid much lower rent than any other tenant in the building because his family knew the landlord. He could take off from work almost whenever he pleased. He took advantage of this freedom because getting away was so easy and often went to visit friends in Philadelphia or New York City.

He also seemed perfectly content in his relationship with Chelsea. The two of them fought, much more lately, but Chelsea figured that was part of adjusting to living with each other and being together around the clock. She could find no reason why Greg wanted to break with reality so much more often than he used to.

Greg's recreational habits had been the source of a big fight the previous night. Tonight Chelsea was hoping for a less confrontational evening. The fight had been a bad one. It had all started when she commented that he was already buzzed when she got home from work at four-thirty in the afternoon. Greg had either opted to take the afternoon off, or more likely, just skipped out early for the day. Officially requesting time off would mean using up vacation time.

"Babe, it's not even five yet. You're what, four beers deep already?" She'd said sitting down next to him on the couch, where he was watching some sci-fi action flick on HBO, beer cans strewn across the coffee and end tables. She hadn't meant it in a confrontational way.

"Sorry, *Mom*," he'd said, "I didn't realize I needed your permission before I started drinking. What's it to you anyway? Just have a beer, it'll lighten you up."

"I don't need to lighten up. I need to pass out for a while and then figure out something to eat for dinner," she said pointedly. Greg merely made a face.

"And I'm not thrilled with being compared to your mother," she added. She made a face. The comparison wasn't even a good one. Greg's mother, Therese, was hardly an example of a strict parent. She pretty much worshipped the ground her son walked on and let him do exactly as he pleased. Still, Chelsea was annoyed, as no girlfriend wants to be compared to her boyfriend's mother.

"So maybe you shouldn't act like her. Jesus, I moved out of my parent's house so I could get away from being nagged, I don't need this from my girlfriend."

"Well, maybe if you stopped acting like a useless frat guy no one would nag you."

This was the wrong thing to say, and from there the disagreement turned into an all-out shouting match, which culminated in Greg hurling the remote control across the room in frustration, where it hit the wall, snapping the plastic off the batteries. Alarmed by Greg's escalating aggression, Chelsea promptly locked herself in the bathroom.

Greg apologized later that night, saying maybe they were both stressed from work and suggested they have a date night. Chelsea smiled weakly through tears, which he kissed and then brushed from her eyes, his strong hands gentle and loving. She figured his tender apology and willingness to work on their relationship was a step in the right direction. Perhaps they were at last on their way back to being on course.

11

✳ ✳ ✳

Technically speaking, Chelsea was only supposed to work until six that night. When she looked at her watch, she saw it said 6:18, and yet she was still waiting for her last table to finish eating so she could drop off their check. They were regulars—an elderly couple who always ordered the same thing: cheeseburger club sandwich on toasted wheat bread (with extra mayo) and mashed potatoes instead of fries for him; lasagna and extra bread for the table for her, always tipped exactly fifteen percent down to the penny. They also always specifically requested Chelsea as their server, so there was really no getting out of it when they walked in the door just before her shift was supposed to end.

Chelsea leaned against the table designated for side work in the kitchen, checking her watch again.

Greg had already been off of work for over an hour and was waiting for her at the apartment. She hoped her table would finish up so she could leave. She did not want another fight with Greg. Tonight was supposed to be a peace-making night, not an opportunity for another blowout. However, things were not looking promising.

It was almost seven by the time Chelsea had finally closed her last check and cashed out with her manager. She drove straight home, but found that the door was locked and Greg was not inside the apartment waiting for her. Since she had taken the car they shared to work, Greg must have gone somewhere with one of his buddies.

Chelsea felt irritated. They had planned a date night; couldn't Greg be at least little understanding? It wasn't her fault that she'd had to stay late at work. She had even snuck away from her side work into the walk-in fridge to send Greg a text message letting him know she was held up at work. Texting on the clock was an offense that, if caught, could cost her one of her shifts. She had risked it to give him a heads up. So where was he?

She picked up her cell and tried calling him. His phone when straight to voicemail which meant he'd turned his phone off. This was his way of making it clear that wherever he was, he was pissed at her. He frequently turned his phone off so that she was unable to reach him and then he stayed out late so she would worry. Chelsea hated when he was passive-aggressive.

In all the time she'd been with Greg, they both had been very open and vocal about what they were thinking and if something was bothering them, rather than pulling passive-aggressive stunts. In the past, neither of them had wanted to purposefully start a fight. Recently though, Greg had started testing her intentionally by doing things he knew would bother her. They would fight, make up, and everything would go back to normal. The routine was getting tiresome, but Chelsea felt that when their relationship was good, it was very good, and it was worth working through any problems to maintain it.

Five hours later she was not so sure. She had waited a while for Greg to come home, but when it was clear that their dinner was not happening, she heated up some leftover Chinese takeout and sat on the couch waiting, hardly tasting her eggrolls. The more time went by, the angrier she got. She watched show after show on television waiting for Greg, and as each show ended and the next one began, she became more annoyed that he had blown her off.

It was after midnight and Chelsea was in the bathroom washing her face and thinking about calling it a night, when she heard Greg coming up the steps to the apartment. He slammed the door behind him and made directly for the kitchen. Chelsea heard him open the fridge and then the unmistakable sound of him cracking open a beer. She took her time in the bathroom. Greg going straight for the alcohol only fueled her anger. She knew they were in for a fight, and was in no rush to start it.

When she finally walked into the living room, she found Greg in front of the television.

He didn't say anything, or in fact, acknowledge her presence at all. After a moment of silence, she spoke.

"So, are you going to tell me where you've been?"

Greg looked over at her. His eyes looked slightly glassy and pinkish.

"I went out," he said. "You didn't come home, so I figured why waste the rest of the night?" He sounded as though he didn't have a care in the world.

"I *did* come home," Chelsea hissed, "I was only an hour late and I told you I got stuck at work! We had plans tonight, remember? You couldn't wait one lousy hour?"

"Listen, babe...I got a call from Trev and he really hooked me up, so I had to go with him to see his guy. Then we hung out and had a few beers, no big deal."

Chelsea blinked. She couldn't believe that the person sitting before her was the guy she'd been with for over two years.

"What do you mean, Trevor 'hooked you up'?" she asked, although she was sure she knew what he had meant.

Greg reached into his pocket and tossed a baggy onto the coffee table. Chelsea didn't have to ask what was in it. He'd had it in the house before when he and Adam were using it, but never this much. Chelsea stared at the baggy.

"Are you insane, bringing an eight ball into our apartment?" she asked. She was fine looking the other way when he and Adam used, but to have Greg there with all that cocaine in their home was more than Chelsea could handle. "Are you trying to get arrested or something?"

"Calm down," Greg said shifting positions on the couch unconcernedly, "Don't be so paranoid. I'm not going to get arrested, why would I get arrested? It's not like the cops do random house searches on the off-chance someone might have coke. I'm not going to tell anyone. You're not going to tell anyone. So what's the big deal? Besides, it won't be here that long, anyway."

"So you're planning on using it all yourself?" Chelsea asked, unable to accept the extent to which she truly no longer knew her boyfriend.

Greg let out a short laugh.

"Why the hell wouldn't I?"

"That's a shit ton of coke. It's going to take you a while to go through it on your own."

"So? All that mean's is I'm set and don't have to worry about getting more for a while. What's it to you, anyway? It's not like you want to share it with me."

"Maybe I just think it would be nice if you weren't rolling all the time. Or drunk."

This was a bold thing to say to Greg. He did not appreciate when she pointed out when he was under the influence of anything, especially since his father had a drinking problem and everyone knew it. To Greg, it was perfectly okay for him to be drunk or high whenever he pleased, but it was not at all okay for anyone else to draw attention to it, Chelsea in particular.

He looked at her sharply, his dark brown eyes boring into her.

"Chels, quit being a pain in the ass."

"How is not wanting drugs in my apartment being a pain in the ass?"

"'Cause it sounds like you're trying to tell me what to do in my own place again and I'm sick of it." Greg was starting to show signs of agitation.

"Oh, please. I'm not telling you what to do and you know it. You just hate that I'm pointing out how you've changed."

Greg rolled his eyes.

"That's right, let's turn this into a discussion about 'our relationship.'" His tone was absolutely dripping with derision.

"What you do affects our relationship. It affects me. And you can't deny that you've changed, Greg."

"What are you talking about? How have I changed?"

"Remember when you actually gave a shit about what I thought and my feelings?" Chelsea felt her throat tighten, but she was determined not to cry. She thought maybe if she held it together he would take her more seriously.

"Give me a break. Chicks always do this, they get all bent out of shape and then try and turn it around like the guy's the one with the problem. Sorry. I'm not interested."

"See, that's exactly what I mean," she said. "You don't give a shit about me or this relationship anymore because it gets in the way of your party-ing, so you can't be bothered." Her eyes were stinging now, but she was still trying to blink back the tears.

Greg looked up at her, his brow furrowed. The glazed look was back and his eyes were unfocused.

"Then what are you with me for, anyway?"

At these words Chelsea felt like she'd gotten the wind knocked out of her.

She sputtered for a moment, and then said "Obviously because I still love you."

"Well," Greg said, "if you love me, then stop acting like my mother and start acting like my girl-friend."

This was not at all the response Chelsea want-ed to hear.

"Good to hear you love me too, Greg," she said coldly.

"Chelsea?"

"Yeah?"

"I thought I told you to quit being a pain in the ass. You're being really stupid right now. Just let it go, and go to bed or something. Damn." Greg's voice was getting louder. Normally Chelsea would back off at this point, but something made her keep pushing.

"Screw you, Greg. God, you're being such an asshole right now."

Greg sat up straight at this.

"I'd watch what you say to me, if I were you," he said, his voice suddenly quiet.

"Or what? Every time I bring up our problems you just get nasty and start yelling. How are we supposed to fix anything if all we do is fight?" Chelsea was raising her voice now.

"Did you ever think that the reason we fight so much is because you're constantly nagging me and telling me what to do? I'm not the one with the problem here. You're the one always finding something to bitch about. When do I come home and give you crap? When am I the one who starts these fights? Never."

Chelsea couldn't believe this. She shook her head in frustration. Of course she always initiated the confrontations, because he had no problem with his lifestyle, she did.

"Well, I'm so sorry for nagging you to be sober for two minutes at a time. I'm sorry I care about how you're not the same guy as the one I started dating. I didn't realize when we moved in together you were turning into a coke head."

At this, Greg got to his feet, crossed the room and got right up in Chelsea's face.

"You better watch what you say to me, little girl," he shouted directly in her ear.

"I've had to watch what I say for months, and I'm sick of it. All your bad moods and hangovers, your sloppy shitfaced nights...I can't keep up with it. I feel like I'm constantly walking on eggshells in my own apartment. What's Greg's mood today? Is he going to flip the fuck out at the smallest thing? Christ, it's like you're a woman!"

"You shut the fuck up!" he shouted. "You think this is all my fault? You're just as much to blame. Maybe if you thought about someone besides yourself and what's inconveniencing you for five seconds..."

"Oh, I thought your problem was I pay too much attention to you like I'm your mother?" Chelsea was yelling right back now.

"Yeah, because you're bitching about how it's not what *you* want or what *you* expect of me!"

"Well excuse me, but I don't think it's too much to want or expect my boyfriend of two years to be able to go a whole week without doing blow or getting drunk out of his mind. Hell, I don't even think I know who you are anymore. I just wonder how many brain cells you've got left after your latest bender!"

SMACK.

It was the last thing she was expecting. Greg slapped Chelsea across the face—hard. She stood in stunned silence for a second, and then said weakly, "Oh my God..."

"I told you to shut the hell up, but you just have to keep on yapping," Greg said, his voice now much softer, but as cold as ice, and more terrifying than his most explosive shout.

Chelsea stood silently for another second, and then ran from the room, out the door, down the wooden steps, and into the night.

12

✶ ✶ ✶

Her heart was pounding wildly. Adrenaline flooded through her body, and she simply ran. Her first instinct: find a place hide. She felt like she was in a dream. She could hear the blood whirring in her ears, and she only had a vague sense that this was actually happening to her. All she knew was that she had to run.

She could not explain why, but she hurdled towards her neighbor's house, and then crept up the steps onto his back deck. She still had never met Alexander Jansson. For all she knew, he could've been an ax murderer, worse than a belligerent boyfriend who had just taken his first swing at his girlfriend's face. Still Chelsea felt she would find shelter on his deck. As quietly as she could given her frenzied state, she tiptoed across the deck, then crouched down and crawled under the picnic table surrounded by mismatched lounge and patio furniture. With any luck, the darkness and furniture would keep her out of sight.

She could hear Greg's yells echoing across the small field that separated Jansson's farmhouse from their apartment. She heard him curse.

"Chelsea, get your ass back here!"

She felt an involuntary sob rise in her throat, and she covered her mouth with her hand to stifle the sound. Greg's yelling was coming closer. His voice, though slurred, was becoming clearer, and moving toward her.

"I swear to God, Chels, you better not go to the cops. Think of what a big *mess* that would be. And who do you think they're gonna believe? You...or me? Half those guys know my Uncle Ray. I could just tell them the eight ball was yours."

Someone in the apartments has to have heard, Chelsea thought, *someone might already have called the police.*

"Come back, Chels! What are you afraid of? Chelsea!"

Her cheek and lip still stung from where he had hit her. They felt fat and burned, for he had slapped her full force and open-handed. Her eyes prickled with tears, and her throat burned, but she kept quiet.

Greg's voice had gotten softer, and he had adopted a sing-song tone.

"Chelsea…I'm not going to hurt you…I just want to talk."

She heard him rustling around some more.

"Come on baby, this whole thing's just a big misunderstanding. Come back! We'll work it out. Come back, baby."

Chelsea still stayed silent. She thought she heard him say "bitch" under his breath.

She heard a muffled sound and heard him curse again. She squinted across the field. He had stumbled in the dark and fallen. She waited to hear him start to call her again, but he did not. Instead his voice got more distant as he mumbled and swore to himself. A few minutes later, she was sure he was gone, probably back into their apartment. A short while afterwards she heard their car's engine start. The car screeched as Greg backed out of the driveway and drove off.

She sat motionless, unsure of what to do next. She couldn't go back to the apartment. Greg would come back. He would be furious, and probably even drunker than during their fight. He had taken the car, so she could not go home to her dad's house, which was across town. She had run out without her cell phone, so she could not call a friend to come pick her up. Instead she stayed crouched under the picnic table on the porch. Her heart still hammered against her ribs. She took sharp gasping breaths as she tried to calm herself and think of what to do next. The lights were off in Jansson's house. It was a little after one in the morning. She was sure no one would answer the door to let a stranger use his phone at this time of night.

Before Chelsea's mind had time to race any further, she heard a voice that made her jerk severely from her seated position under the table.

"Would you care to come inside?"

It was Jansson, standing on the other side of the screen door. She had not heard him walking toward her, had not seen movement for he had not turned on any lights. She was listening so intently to where Greg was that she didn't even notice Jansson open his back door.

"Are you alright?" he asked when she didn't respond.

His voice was gentle; cautious. He had a very slight accent that she couldn't place, perhaps from somewhere in Eastern Europe, she supposed. Chelsea did not move, half out of humiliation and half out of concern that a stranger had invited her inside. She had yet to rule out the possibility that he was an ax murderer.

"I'm terribly sorry," he said with a small embarrassed smile, "but I seem to have overheard something just now."

She wondered whether he meant the entire fight with Greg, or Greg's drunken yells into the night while searching for her in the darkness.

"Please," she said at last, her voice quivering, "Please don't call the police. It was just a misunderstanding..." She thought of her earlier wish that someone might have called the cops. Now she didn't want that. Officer Sciaruto might be the one to show up. He would surely tell her father and Chelsea couldn't face Gene right now. Not like this.

Jansson looked at her curiously, his brow furrowed slightly.

"I think I understand better than you realize. Please, come inside. You can use the phone. It's cold out there. I promise I'm harmless." His face was earnest, his pale eyes crinkled in a welcoming smile, as if to say *I'm not an ax murderer, and I'm certainly not going to hit you across the face.*

Without knowing why, Chelsea rose, and followed the professor inside the house.

Jansson had been up late grading papers and had fallen asleep on his Lay-Z-Boy chair. He was awakened by raised voices coming from one of the apartments next door. Not sure exactly what he was hearing, and unable to make out the words, he could unmistakably pick up on the emotions. Jansson turned off his lamp so he could see better in the dark outside, and went to the window, peering across the field. A few moments later he heard a door slam and saw the figure of a young woman run down the steps and out into the darkness. The moon was bright, so he could see reasonably well. The young woman stalled at first, unsure of where to run, but then made for his house, creeping up the back steps and crawling underneath his patio table.

Jansson immediately started trying to locate his cell phone to call the police, but he couldn't find it. He thought he left it upstairs in the pocket of the slacks he had worn that day, but he did not want to go fetch it. He stayed put where he could see both the frightened young woman and the man angrily chasing after her. He figured if it came down to it, he would step outside and come between the two. Jansson was six foot four, broad-shouldered, and would make an intimidating adversary for the young man if he pursued the girl onto Jansson's property.

To his relief, the young man gave up rather quickly and drunkenly made his way back up to his apartment. When he saw the car pull away, he debated calling the police, as the driver was visibly intoxicated, but he felt the more pressing matter was to confront the teen hiding on his deck.

Chelsea now sat at the small kitchen table while Jansson made her some herbal tea. She didn't like tea but accepted his offer to make her a cup. She could not speak for a few minutes, but she felt an urgent need to explain herself to the professor. She did not know him at all, but he had shown her a kindness, and she felt he deserved to know why she had come onto his deck and involved him in her nightmare. She also felt the inexplicable need to excuse her boyfriend's behavior.

"We got into another fight," she said the second he put down the tea in front of her. "He's drunk and I think he did coke tonight, and I should have never confronted him when he's like that. He gets mean when he does coke." She didn't know why she was telling a total stranger about her boyfriend's drug use. She simply felt that she needed to justify the situation.

Jansson did not respond to her mention of cocaine, but instead settled himself across the table and gave her an appraising look. Then he asked seriously, "Does he hit you often?"

Chelsea's hand flew up to her face. She had forgotten her fat lip and raw cheek where angry red welts in the exact shape of a hand now rose. She couldn't deny it now.

"Never before tonight," she said.

Jansson nodded and mumbled something that sounded like "Ah hah." He then said, "And you're sure you don't want me to phone for the police?"

Chelsea shook her head. "No, that would make things worse."

She expected Jansson to protest, to try and convince her it was the right thing to do, to turn Greg in, and have him arrested, but he said nothing.

The truth was that Jansson had known his fair share of young girls like Chelsea, in abusive relationships, not necessarily physical abuse, but certainly girls who were ultimately controlled by a boyfriend. He also knew most of them were too scared to report their boyfriends, or had such low self-esteem that they believed they deserved the abuse and that they would not be able find anyone else to love them. He was not about to push this young woman into doing anything at the moment. All too often, the women would go back to their boyfriends. It was all they knew. Jansson decided he was not going to do anything that would result in Chelsea going back to the inebriated son of a bitch who had just struck her in the face and then chased her out of her own apartment.

Chelsea was grateful. She didn't think she could stand having to recount the night's events to the police. She didn't even want to think about what had happened, even though the screaming and the sharp, hot pain she felt on her face and in her heart when Greg had slapped her was all she could think about.

He let her sit in silence for a several minutes. He busied himself in the kitchen cleaning and organizing, glancing at Chelsea every so often to see how she was doing. Then when she looked as though she might try to leave, he tried to put her at ease.

"I apologize; I haven't really introduced myself yet, have I?"

He held out a hand to her.

"I'm Alexander Jansson. We've been neighbors for a while now,

haven't we?"

Chelsea nodded, taking his hand. His grip was gentle. "I'm Chelsea Shepherd. I've been living in the apartment for just over a year."

He had pronounced his last name *YAHN-son*. Chelsea had assumed it was pronounced *JAN-sen* when she had delivered his mail to him weeks ago. She'd had no idea then that he was foreign.

His first name was Alexander. She thought of the only other Alexander in her life, the brother she had never met.

"How old are you, Chelsea?" Jansson asked, surveying her. Chelsea got the distinct impression that he did not want to hear more about Greg. He also looked mildly concerned, as though he thought she might be under eighteen.

"Nineteen," she said.

"Do you go to school around here?"

"No, I'm not a student," she said.

Typically, when someone asked about her status as a student (or in her case, a non-student) Chelsea became defensive and irritated. Yet she somehow sensed that Jansson was trying to reach out to her by making conversation, getting to know her, and trying to make her feel comfortable in a very strange and awkward situation. Still, for reasons she could not explain, even to herself, she felt she could trust him. She wondered why a complete stranger seemed so protective of her. His concern for her safety did not seem to be a cause for alarm, nor did he seem to have any inappropriate interest in her. Rather, he gave the impression of being genuinely concerned for the welfare of another human being, particularly one so young who had just been slapped.

"I only ask because you look to be about the age of my students. I teach at the University of Scranton."

Chelsea knew two or three of her high school classmates who were currently students there. She wondered if he knew any of them.

There was an awkward silence.

"Can I ask where your accent is from?" Chelsea said lamely, trying to make conversation.

"Sweden. That's where I'm from. Though my accent has considerably lessened in the fifteen years I've been in the States. Or so I'm told." Jansson smiled.

Chelsea forced a weak smile in return.

"Is there someone I can call for you?" Jansson was starting to look a bit uncomfortable. He had offered Chelsea assistance during her crisis, but he hadn't thought of what to do once the immediate danger was over.

"I left my phone in the apartment...it has all my friends' numbers in it," Chelsea said.

"What about family? You can't call your parents' house?"

Chelsea squirmed slightly in her seat.

"I can't call my dad right now. It's the middle of the night, and he'll freak out. Then he'll insist on calling the police and pressing charges, and I can't—I just can't deal with that right now. Everything's happening way too fast."

"Well," said Jansson slowly, "would you like me to go over to the apartment with you to get your phone?"

Chelsea thought for a moment. Truthfully her brain didn't seem to be functioning on a normal level. Her mind seemed to be oscillating between thinking in slow motion and then racing faster than she could handle. She didn't know what she planned to do next, but she knew it wasn't going to include going back into that apartment and risk seeing Greg again, even when accompanied by a large Swede.

Finally Jansson spoke.

"Tell you what. Why don't you sleep on the couch tonight and we'll figure out how to help you first thing in the morning. Alright?"

Slowly Chelsea nodded. She knew that it was odd to accept such an offer from a complete stranger. Jansson knew it was odd to make such an offer to a complete stranger. Yet there didn't seem to be anything else they could do for the moment, and as strange as the situation was, neither Chelsea nor Jansson seemed to be too concerned.

"Thank you," Chelsea said.

"Not at all," Jansson replied.

13

✳ ✳ ✳

Jansson now sat in his Lay-Z-Boy chair in quiet
contemplation over the situation before him.
He couldn't seem to quiet his mind. Someone
whom he'd never met until an hour ago was
going to be sleeping on his couch. He didn't know
quite what to make of why he'd offered to help so
quickly, just that in the moment he knew it was the
right thing to do. All he knew was that Chelsea,
this nineteen-year-old, was no different from the
young women who sat in his lectures every day.
He knew how the situation might look to an out-
sider; a middle-aged man offering asylum to a
nineteen-year old girl. Even though he had the
purest of intentions where his guest was concerned, he worried that the situation might get

sticky. What would the girl's father say? Would he be mad when he found out that Jansson hadn't insisted she call home rather than stay with a stranger, and an older man besides?

He believed very strongly in a solid line between a student and a teacher, and firmly maintained that an older man should never take advantage of a young woman. Throughout his time as a professor, he had certainly encountered other faculty members who were inappropriately involved with their students. He disapproved of these relationships and was generally put off by the professors that were said to have used sexual intimidation on their female students. Jansson believed the role of a teacher was sacred. A teacher was there for guidance and education, someone who a student could admire and respect; a teacher was not there to pursue his students sexually or romantically.

This almost knee-jerk instinct to put a professional and platonic distance between himself and his young female students stemmed from a long academic career both as a student himself, and later as a faculty member during which time he had witnessed male academics abusing their position of authority.

When Jansson was fourteen, he had been in a *Samhällsorientering* class, the Swedish equivalent to a secondary school social studies course, which was taught by a man called Nyström. At the time, Nyström was in his late thirties, and sported what most of the students referred to as a "pervy mustache". He was thin with long waxy fingers and a sharp mind. He gave engaging and informative lectures, had a genial personality, and paid very close, unwanted attention to the female students, particularly the pretty ones.

Several weeks into the first term, Jansson and the other students began to notice special attention that Nyström was paying to the girls. While he called on both the boys and girls indiscriminately, he seemed to frequently find cause to ask the girls to come by after class for extra help with an assignment, and sometimes during lectures he would look straight at one girl, even if she hadn't been speaking, for several minutes before looking up at the class as a whole, as though jerking from a trance. His voice, however, stayed steady and informative.

Nyström would also take any opportunity to touch a female student. Although he was careful to never do so in an overtly inappropriate way, it was still unnecessary physical contact none-the-less. When the class would sit at their desks working on projects or copying notes from textbooks, Nyström would lean over a girl's shoulder appearing to be checking her work while resting both his hands on either side of the girl's desk. This seemed to Jansson like a clear and unnecessary invasion of the girls' personal space, but as Nyström was doing it in front of the whole class, he didn't seem to think he was crossing any boundaries. Everyone knew Nyström stood a little too close and obviously favored he girls, but they didn't think much of it. Jansson, however, stayed especially cognizant of all the interactions Nyström had with his female classmates.

In Nyström's class, Jansson sat next to a girl named Katja. Katja had long, silky red-brown hair, snow-white skin, and an adorable patch of freckles across her nose and underneath her violet eyes, reminiscent of a young Elizabeth Taylor. At some point or another most of the boys in Jansson's year had been sweet on Katja as she was pretty, smart, and nice to everyone. Jansson had known her since they were ten and the two were very friendly. It wasn't until Nyström started so blatantly favoring Katja that Jansson began to have serious concerns. As she sat only one desk over from him, Jansson frequently saw Nyström leaning over her seat while she worked. During class discussions, his eyes would linger on her for long moments after she had finished answering a question he'd posed, and when she raised her hand to contribute to the class, he frequently had taken to leaving the front of the classroom and standing right in front of her desk.

Katja complained to Jansson in hushed tones after class about how uncomfortable Nyström was making her feel.

"The way he stares at me for so long, it makes me feel sick," she'd said. "And when he's leaning over the desk, I feel like I can't move. He blocks me in."

"Do you think we should tell someone?" Jansson asked.

"What could they do? Tell him he can't make eye contact with the girls in the class? I don't know. I don't like him."

Then one day when the class was hard at work composing their history essays, Nyström moved away from the desk of a blonde girl whose notes he had just been checking, and once again leaned over Katja as she worked. The other students, with their heads bent down, scribbling furiously at their essays did not look up, but Jansson happened to glance over just as Nyström lightly brushed a strand of Katja's long hair back behind her ear. Katja continued writing vigilantly as though she didn't notice, but Jansson could see her body tense up and her porcelain cheeks begin to flush. The next week when Nyström asked her to stop by after school to review her paper, Katja begged Jansson to come with her.

"Please, Alexander!" she implored him, her arms crossed as though she were bracing her body for a fall. "Don't leave me alone with him."

Jansson didn't need convincing.

He accompanied Katja to Nyström's classroom after school let out and stood expectantly by the door so it was clear he was waiting for her. At Katja's request, he was also carrying her books so Nyström might think the two were going out. Unsurprisingly, Nyström didn't look too pleased to see that Katja had brought a friend. He kept his distance and went over her paper in less than ten minutes, leading Jansson to conclude that there was no real reason for them to discuss the essay in the first place; it was merely a way for Nyström to get her alone in the classroom. After the meeting was over, when Katja reached the door where Jansson was standing, Jansson instinctively grabbed her hand and put on his best fourteen-year-old protective boyfriend face.

Katja thanked Jansson and the two continued to act visibly chummy in front of Nyström for the rest of the term, carrying on the charade that Katja had a watchful boyfriend sitting next to her. Nyström, for his part, must have realized his special attention to Katja was drawing more eyes than he wanted, and began to distribute his attention for the other girls in the class more evenly. He did, however, continue to hover around the girls' desks.

A few years afterward, Jansson's mother, unaware of Nyström's past questionable behavior, mentioned to her son that she'd heard through the grapevine that Nyström had resigned his position at Jansson's old school.

"Apparently there was some business with him and one of his female students!" she reported one day when he was home from university for the summer holidays. Mrs. Jansson was very well-connected and could always be counted on to get the full scoop.

"They gave him an ultimatum. Resign, or they'd fire him," she continued.

"Well it's about time," Jansson had said.

During his time attending university, Jansson had heard rumors of certain professors who would socialize with their students outside of the classroom. Some of them would just meet their students in a local pub for informal intellectual and philosophical discussions over a pint. Other, less scrupulous faculty members would try to covertly date one or more of their female students. None of the rumors were ever substantiated by the university, which did not condone such relationships, but young coeds would often brag about their trysts with certain good-looking professors. One student Jansson knew from around campus drunkenly admitted one night at a party that she had been sleeping with her philosophy professor all fall term and they had split just before finals. Suddenly her A-minus average had turned into a C in the class for the term.

"So who the fuck knows what grade I actually earned?" she had slurred to a group of students.

Jansson was just as put off by teachers who had romantic or sexual relationships with their students as he was by teachers making unwanted advances towards the young coeds. Even if the relationship was consensual, Jansson believed that a faculty member dating a student was unethical, untoward, and it unfairly skewed the way the professor graded his girlfriend for better or worse.

When Jansson arrived at the University of Scranton, he received his fair share of attention from the female student body. One of his colleagues teased him and informed him that in addition to receiving an above average ranking as an instructor on a popular website that rate's college professors, Alexander Jansson was rated as being "hot" as well, which was apparently an aspect of the rating system only bestowed on the faculty members who students considered to be lust-worthy.

Jansson was embarrassed by this distinction. Of course he was somewhat flattered, but he would rather his lasting impression on his students be for challenging them and imparting knowledge and wisdom, not for being "a hunk".

"Don't sweat it," one of the other psychology professors named Dr. Rabinovitz, a portly, smiley woman in her late fifties with a long, frizzy, gray braid down her back, had told him. "You're a good-looking guy, a bunch of college girls are bound to notice. Trust me; they're not taking an abnormal psychology class to meet dreamy older men." She'd laughed.

"All the same," Jansson had protested, "I'd rather they choose to take my abnormal psych section over Dr. Phelps' section because they like my class better, not my appearance."

"It's the accent," Dr. Rabinovitz had joked.

It was true that Professor Alexander Jansson did have the reputation of being one of the more "dreamy" instructors on campus. His mesmerizing blue eyes, his smooth, perfect skin and pale blonde hair coupled with his touch of mysteriousness that came with being foreign, specifically Scandinavian, did seem to drive some of the young women he taught wild. Certain sections of his classes were disproportionately female, and most of the young women in his lectures were eager to participate in class discussions, hoping to gain his notice and attention for a few short minutes. While most of the female students in his 8:00 a.m. lectures wore sweats and messy buns to class, all of his other classes were filled with girls who were fully made up, wearing stylish clothing, often more low-cut than necessary given the setting. As he was quite the man-about-campus, he knew that this was not the norm for class-going outfits.

Far more female than male students visited Jansson during his office hours to discuss upcoming tests and to review papers. This was not to say that Jansson did not have students who took his classes for all the right reasons and had their eyes on the ball, so to speak. Never the less, even some of his most studious, academically-oriented female students would sometimes blush when he called on them in class.

Jansson took all this with a grain of salt. What mattered to him was that his students were getting the most academically out of his courses, and though he never looked at the professor rating website, Dr. Rabinovitz assured him that the majority of his students had overwhelmingly positive things to say about his teaching and curriculum, in addition to finding him "hot."

"Gee, thanks a lot, Deborah," he'd told her.

Jansson did enjoy his students and found happiness in participating in school-sponsored student groups and events. He helped organize the Cancer Walk each year and was one of the faculty advisors to the international students club. He also worked with the student government to help find speakers to come to campus. Overall he was pretty satisfied with his life and his students in the university community.

Jansson now surveyed Chelsea in his kitchen. Chelsea was not one of his students, but she was exactly the age of the kids he taught. Yes, they were over eighteen and not technically kids, but there was a big difference between a fully independent young adult and a college kid, safe within the confines of a major university. Based on first impressions, Jansson would have placed Chelsea squarely in the latter category, yet he saw her somewhat differently from the coeds who sat in his psychology classes. There was something about her that seemed much older than a college student, but at the same time, something that was young and vulnerable about her. She had a strength and calmness in her that made it hard for him to believe she was only nineteen, yet somewhere behind her eyes, in her movements, he could see fear and doubt, as thought she was just a small child waiting for God himself to reach out to take her by the hand.

He glanced over at the young woman sitting in his home. For an instant the image of her body flashed in his mind. She was, after all, quite lovely, and he was, after all, only human. For a moment his eyes lingered on her form, her skin, her hair. But as quickly as this image had appeared, he had pushed it to the very back of his mind. For now, he only felt a feeling of fatherly tenderness, reaching out to the lost young person.

She had curled up on one of his couches. He removed a folded orange and brown knitted afghan that smelled like cloves from the back of the easy chair and placed it on her legs, not quite laying it over her, but giving her an invitation to use it. She quietly unfolded the afghan and wrapped it around her, closing her eyes. Although he had walked away, Chelsea sensed that Jansson had not left the room. Yet somehow, she felt that he was not watching her, but rather watching over her. Comforted, she felt herself slowly drifting off to sleep.

ℭℜ

Early the next morning, Jansson was hesitant to wake Chelsea, who was still asleep on his couch. He didn't want to leave her alone in the house without discussing the situation.

He gently touched her shoulder.

Chelsea opened her eyes. It took her half a second to remember where she was and what had happened the night before. She sat up abruptly.

"No need to worry," Jansson said. "You can stay here while I'm at work, and tonight we'll try and figure out what to do next, alright?"

"Alright," Chelsea said uncertainly. She was so tired and was having trouble thinking.

"Feel free to go back to sleep," Jansson added as her turned to leave. "I know it's early. Help yourself to anything in the kitchen if you get hungry. I'll see you later."

He walked out to his car wondering if Chelsea would be there when he return.

14

✲ ✲ ✲

Greg awoke that morning with severe cotton mouth. He looked at the clock radio next to the bed. It was almost noon. Sunlight streamed through the blinds with a powerful vengeance, making him groan and pull the pillow over his head. The previous night was a complete blur. After some trepidation, he got out of bed and kicked an empty beer can on his way to the kitchen. He drank two tall glasses of water and tried to think.

It was Friday. He should have been at work three hours ago. He looked around the kitchen in search of his cell phone, but it was nowhere in sight. He moved his search to the living room and after some rummaging, recovered his phone from between the couch cushions. He had several missed calls and a voicemail, all from his uncle. He didn't bother to listen to the message; he was sure he knew what it said. He dialed his uncle's number. It picked up halfway through the first ring.

"Uncle Ray, it's Greg."

"Gregory. Are you having some kind of emergency or are you stranded somewhere?"

"Nah, Uncle Ray, I just…"

"Then is there a halfway decent reason why your ass isn't at work yet?"

Greg rubbed his eyes and groaned.

"Listen kid, I'm okay with you coming in late every once in a while, but I'd appreciate a little notice if you're not going to show up at all," his uncle responded curtly.

"Yeah, I'm sorry about that Uncle Ray, Chelsea and I went out to eat last night and I think I got some bad seafood or something 'cause I was up all night puking my guts out. I only just woke up, and I was on the floor in the bathroom. I'm sorry, man. I should have called and left a message last night that I would need to come in late today." Greg was a professional smooth talker. He had all the charm and self-assuredness he needed to have just about anybody eating out of the palm of his hand. Lying came easily to him, and it was even easier over the phone when he didn't have to try and look contrite.

His uncle sighed.

"Don't worry about it, but next time, give us a heads-up. You coming in today, or are you still puking?"

"I think I'll be alright to come in for the rest of the day"

"Alright. I better see you soon..."

"Twenty minutes, man."

Greg hung up the phone but didn't move from the couch. He was still unsure of what had taken place last night. He remembered going over to Adam's house and taking shots, and then he remembered driving back to the apartment and passing out around 3:00 a.m. But he couldn't remember much before that. He got up and had another drink of water. He poured himself a big bowl of cereal and sat at the table eating it, trying to piece together the puzzle of the previous night. He popped two aspirin and drank another glass of water.

Things were getting a little clearer now. He remembered Chelsea wasn't home over an hour after her shift was supposed to end. He remembered drinking a few beers and then being picked up by his friends, Trevor and Jesse, when he was sick of waiting for Chelsea to get home. The three of them had gone back to Jesse's house.

The events of the previous night slowly began to come back to him. After a few more beers they went to Trevor's connection's house, some sketchy white trash place a few towns over. Luckily for them the guy had just gotten some new product and gave Greg a pretty discount on an eight ball as a first time customer. Greg usually didn't make transactions through dealers. He often chose instead to give his friends money to get his coke for him, or used Adam's coke when it was his turn to buy. Now that he had seen how easy the deal was, he figured he would utilize Trevor's connection for future transactions.

After that, they had gone back to Trevor's house, drank some more beers and sampled their purchases. Eventually he had decided to head back to the apartment. He had work the next morning so he figured he would go home, maybe take a quick hot shower then go right to sleep.

But when he'd gotten home, Chelsea was there, ready for a fight. He remembered arguing with her, her nagging him, and when he told her to stop being a pain in the ass. His head really hurt now. Then he remembered her running out of the apartment in the middle of the night. He remembered chasing after her, calling her name but not being able to find her.

What had made her run outside in the middle of the fight? He tried to recall the argument. Then the memory of reaching out and striking her hit him with a jolt of sudden sobriety.

"Shit..." he said softly to himself.

Greg had never hit Chelsea before. He'd gotten into physical fights with other guys, usually during a drunken stupor, but he had never raised a hand toward her or any other woman in his life.

Both shock at his own actions and confusion as to where Chelsea was now riddled his already parched and aching brain. He hadn't been able to find her after she ran out so he went to Adam's for a few hours before coming home and passing out. So where was she now? She couldn't be at work. Chelsea always worked Friday nights, not day shifts.

He poured himself a final glass of water, downed it in a matter of seconds, and then went to shower and get dressed for work. He would have to try and sort things out with Chelsea later that night. Trying to shake off his feeling of uneasiness, he got in his car and pulled away from the apartment.

It was only after she was sure that Greg had left for work that Chelsea considered trying to reenter her apartment to grab some of her belongings, especially her phone and her purse. She got to the top of the stairs and tried to open the door, but it was locked. Whether Greg was hung over and not thinking, or he had done it on purpose out of spite, he had locked her out. He had to know she had not grabbed her keys when she ran out during their fight.

She returned to Jansson's kitchen and tried to figure out her next move. She was thankful she did not have work at all that day after having traded shifts with one of the other girls. She was relieved she wouldn't have to call in and explain her situation. She could hardly go into the restaurant and wait tables with no work clothes and a black and blue face.

She picked up Jansson's portable phone and dialed one of the only numbers she knew by heart. It was the first number she always called when she was sick and needed her shift covered at the restaurant, and the number she had called the last time she and Greg had gotten into a fight and needed to get out of the house.

Less than an hour later, a rather beat-up-looking tan Volkswagen pulled into Jansson's driveway. Brooke worked at Mountain Range

Grille with Chelsea. Brooke was three years older than her, and had a two-year-old daughter. If anyone could help in a serious boyfriend crisis, it was Brooke. Although she was two inches shorter and ten pounds lighter than Chelsea, who was only five-three herself, she was what Chelsea considered one tough chick. She lived with her boyfriend and their baby daughter, and had been taking care of herself since she was fifteen years old. Brooke was more than capable of holding her own and was, as far as Chelsea could tell, fearless.

Brooke wasted no time in prompting Chelsea to explain the events of the previous night in minute detail.

"Alright, spill," she said marching right up the steps onto the porch and eyeing Chelsea's injured face over her sunglasses.

The y talked for an hour, during which Brooke agreed to pick up Chelsea's remaining shifts for the week or get them covered for her.

"So this is it, right?" Brooke said stonily. "Game over. He hits you, he's done."

"Right," Chelsea said, somewhat taken aback. She hadn't actually thought about what last night meant for her relationship. Were they broken up now? She thought about it for a moment more, and then said firmly. "I'm not going back to him."

"Good," said Brooke, looking satisfied.

She told Chelsea that the first place Greg would look for her was at work, so she should lay low for a while. The two agreed that Brooke would tell the manager not to schedule Chelsea for any shifts until further notice. Brooke was to explain to the boss that Chelsea had mono, possibly even pneumonia and that she would contact the restaurant when she was healthy enough to work again.

"If they want a doctor's note or something, I'll cross that bridge when I get to it." Chelsea said.

"Yeah, for sure. Okay, that's settled; let's see what we can do about getting into your apartment so you can get your stuff," Brooke said, matter-of-factly.

"What?" Chelsea asked, confused. "It's locked, I can see my keys sitting on the table from the window."

Apparently this was not terribly concerning for Brooke.

"Honey, a locked door is just a speed bump."

Without missing a beat, Brooke marched out the door and across the field between Jansson's house and the apartment, walked up the stairs, and started fiddling with the door handle. Chelsea followed close behind, torn between curiosity about how Brooke was planning to break into the apartment, and apprehension that Greg might suddenly return home unexpectedly.

Between two bobby-pins, a debit card and a paper clip, Brooke had the door unlocked in ninety seconds flat. She pushed the door open a few inches, and stared up at Chelsea from her knees and said, "There you go, let's go get your stuff."

"Where exactly did you pick up that handy little skill?" Chelsea asked, raising an eyebrow at her friend.

"Don't worry about it," Brooke said, pushing open the door the rest of the way. "Another story for another day."

As quickly as possible, the two packed a large duffel bag of Chelsea's clothes, makeup, and some toiletries. She also grabbed her wallet, her purse, and her phone, almost forgetting the phone charger until Brooke pointed to the outlet into which it was plugged. Since Greg and Chelsea shared the car, Chelsea had no way of getting around while she was staying in Jansson's house, for however long that was, but she had the feeling that it was alright to stay with him, at least temporarily. Brooke drove her to the ATM so she could get some cash to tide her over. They stopped for some iced coffees, and then returned back to Jansson's house.

"Alright hon," Brooke said, rummaging through her purse for her cigarettes, "I've gotta get home. Wade's at home with Quinn, and he probably hasn't put her down for a nap yet." She looked

Chelsea right in the face. "You call me if you need anything else, okay?"

Chelsea promised, and Brooke gave her a quick but tight hug before driving off and leaving Chelsea alone with her thoughts in the empty house until Jansson returned after his final class of the day.

What Chelsea did not know is that later that evening when Brooke went in for the dinner shift, she asked to speak with the manager, Russ, alone. While in Russ's office, Brooke twisted her thick, dark brown hair back into a messy bun as she explained to him how she would be covering Chelsea's last two shifts of the week, and that Chelsea would be unable to work for a while. But instead of telling her boss that Chelsea had mono or pneumonia as they had discussed, she chose a lie a little closer to the truth.

"Her strung-out boyfriend beat her up last night. She's staying with friends until we can convince her to press charges, but for now she's trying to stay under the radar so the piece of shit can't find her and clobber her again."

Russ, who was decent human being despite all evidence to the contrary, surprised Brooke by his response. He usually did his best to hide the fact that he was actually a good guy by being a hard-ass.

"I'll have to rearrange the schedule a little bit but that's fine. She has a job here when she's ready to come back," Russ said. "And you'll have to tell me what this boyfriend looks like and tell the other girls to let me know if he comes in looking for her."

"Okay. Why?"

"Just let me know. I might have words with him if I see him."

Brooke raised her eyebrows at her manager, but felt relieved.

"Alright I've got to go clock in. Thanks for being cool about all this."

"You bet."

"And this is just between us," Brooke said sharply as she turned to leave the office.

"So long as that creep stays out of my restaurant," he called after her.

With Chelsea's job secured, Brooke walked out the kitchen door and went to smoke one last cigarette before her starting her shift.

15

★ ★ ★

Just as Brooke predicted, the restaurant was the first place Greg expected to find Chelsea. When she didn't come home the night after their fight, he assumed she was crashing with a friend.

He called her cell phone over and over but she didn't answer. He left her two messages asking her to call him back but never heard back from her. He even called her father's house, but hung up when Gene answered. He noticed many of her personal belongings were no longer in the apartment. Clothes were missing and her makeup, toothbrush and hairdryer were gone. He understood why she was staying somewhere else, but he at least expected her to talk to him, to let him explain or apologize. If nothing else, he deserved a goodbye or a confirmation from her that she was not planning on coming back.

After a weekend of no word from Chelsea, he stopped into Mountain Range Grille hoping to find her working or talk to someone who could tell him where she was staying. To his frustration, she wasn't working when he got there, and all the other two servers would tell him was, "She's not in today."

"Well, can you tell me what days she is scheduled to work this week?" Greg asked.

"I'm not sure," said the first server, who was tall and freckly with rare naturally blonde tresses. She shrugged, then mumbled something about her food being up and briskly walked away.

"What about you," he turned to the other server, a pretty twentysomething with a long auburn ponytail and a purple fabric headband.

"You'll have to ask a manager," she said. "We're not supposed to give out that sort of information."

"Look, I'm her boyfriend. I live with her. It's not like I'm some crazy off the street."

"I'll get a manager for you," she replied, and she headed toward the kitchen, flipping her ponytail over her shoulder as she swiftly walked away, though not before Greg had checked out her butt as soon as her back was turned.

Greg was getting irritated. He knew the schedule must be around here somewhere, how hard was it for someone to just look at it and tell him when his own girlfriend was working? He stood awkwardly near the door for a few minutes, chewing on his thumb nail. Finally the manager came out of the kitchen and walked up to him.

"I hear you're inquiring about Chelsea?"

"Yeah, she's my girlfriend. I just want to know the next day she's working."

The manager furrowed his brows.

"We can't give out our server's schedules," he said. "If she's your girlfriend I'm surprised she hasn't told you her schedule herself."

Smartass prick, Greg thought, and opened his mouth to say something scathing to the manager, but the manager cut him off saying "All I can tell you is that she's not on the schedule this week so I can't tell you when she'll be in next."

"Aren't you the one who makes the schedule?"

"Sometimes. This week the Assistant GM is doing it, and he's not in today."

"So what, I'm just supposed to stop in again next week and keep trying to catch her on a shift?"

"I wouldn't suggest that," said the manager. "The best I can do is let her know that you stopped in next time she works."

Greg rolled his eyes.

"Thanks, you've been a real big help, pal."

He turned and walked out of the restaurant.

"Have a nice day," Russ said to Greg's retreating figure.

When Jansson returned home after that first day, he told Chelsea he had thought long and hard about the situation, and that if she didn't mind the arrangement, she could stay with him until she was ready to call her father and report Greg to the police. Chelsea did not care much for the idea of calling either her dad or the cops, but she was content with having a place to stay, so she agreed. For now, staying with Jansson seemed like the best decision she could make without actually having to make a decision.

Greg had been calling, leaving voice messages, and texting her for days, but she ignored his calls and deleted his voicemails without listening to them. She didn't want to hear what he had to say, and didn't trust herself not to run right back to him if he said something charming and apologetic. He was very charismatic when he wanted to be. After a few days, his attempts to reach her became fewer and farther between, and often Chelsea simply kept her phone on silent. For the time being, she wanted to put Greg out of her mind.

Both Jansson and Chelsea worried privately that their new living situation would be awkward or uncomfortable. However, they were pleasantly surprised to find that they swiftly fell into an easy routine. Each morning he woke up and headed to work. Chelsea slept in, and then got up to do chores. She did laundry, cleaning, and odd jobs around the house. She kept herself busy raking leaves and walking to the closest Qwick-Mart if ever Jansson needed anything. She also liked to take long walks in the afternoons. She wanted to keep active and could only stand being cooped up in the house for so long.

Chelsea often made dinner for the two of them, which they would enjoy together when he returned home after his classes. Usually he would retreat into his office to get work done and grade papers and tests for a few hours while Chelsea watched television. After he was done working they would watch a movie together or play cards. Sometimes he would tell her about what he was teaching in his classes. She told him about her family, her job, and how she used to be a dancer. On the weekends Jansson would let Chelsea take his car for a few hours to get groceries, meet a friend for coffee, or go to the mall. Sometimes he would accompany her to the store. Chelsea was careful to go to the market in the next town over so she wouldn't risk running into her father or Greg.

After a short while, neither Chelsea nor Jansson felt any awkwardness about their situation. There was an understanding between them that was a strange comfort for them both. Before she knew it, Chelsea had been living with Jansson for a few weeks. She felt as close to happy as she had been in a long time.

She didn't even mind when Jansson encouraged her to take some classes at Scranton.

"I think there are some courses offered that you would find very interesting," he'd said over dinner one night.

"I can't afford any classes right now," Chelsea explained. "Although I'm sure my dad would be so thrilled to get me on a college campus that he'd pay for any class I wanted to take."

"Why is it you *aren't* in college?"

Jansson had been wondering this for a while. Chelsea was bright and conversational, and he couldn't see why a young woman with such potential would rather work a less-than-minimum-wage job and live with a deadbeat boyfriend than be off at school getting an education and partying with the rest of the kids her age.

As always, this was a touchy subject for Chelsea. It had been a major source of conflict with her parents. Now, over a year after announcing to them that college was not right for her, she couldn't remember what her reasoning had been for passing it up.

"I don't know..." she said. "I guess I don't know what I want to do with my life, so committing to a major doesn't seem right."

"Well you should take a few classes in different subjects and see what interests you," Jansson suggested.

"Maybe," was all Chelsea could think to say before quickly changing the subject.

16

★ ★ ★

When Jansson first moved to the states, he was thirty-seven. Although it would have been more practical to buy a condo or rent an apartment since it was just him living alone, what he really wanted was his own house. He wanted to feel at home and not like he was just going to be at Scranton temporarily. He always liked feeling that he could spread out in his own space; a condo would have been claustrophobic and stifling. Furthermore, he couldn't see a condo without thinking about showy waterfront one Margit was now living in with their son and a new man. *No*, he thought. *Condos are for chumps.* Living in an apartment building would leave him with even less space, and was always a gamble because you never knew how loud your neighbors might turn out to be. So when he found the Foothills farmhouse in the real estate section of the paper, he contacted the realtor immediately.

He had barely crossed the threshold of the house during the showing when he knew he could feel at home there. He made an offer later that afternoon. The house was perfectly within his price range, particularly because it was in a quiet farming town well outside of Scranton and other big cities in Pennsylvania, and he even managed to negotiate a lower than asking price on the sale.

Yes, Jansson was quite satisfied with his new home. He knew that he didn't need all the square footage and more than one bedroom, but, he reasoned, you never know. He was still young and there was plenty of time to meet someone with whom he might someday want to share his house. He knew of course he wasn't ready to date yet. He had just ended his marriage and figured it would take some time before he was ready to "get back out there" where his love life was concerned. He was still smarting from finding out that Margit had been having an affair and had effectively alienated him from his own son, so the idea of opening up to someone and putting his trust in a woman didn't seem altogether appealing to him at the moment.

He hadn't counted on this aversion to relationships to last quite as long as it did. Two years went by before his loneliness finally overpowered his desire to stay emotionally closed off from all relationships. He went on a handful of first dates that didn't pan out into anything serious, but, he figured, at least he was back on the dating horse. One advantage to working at a major university was that someone always knew someone else who was single, and Jansson's coworker friends were more than happy to set him up. In their minds it was a shame that a man like Alexander Jansson wasn't seeing anyone.

The year Jansson turned forty he met a woman named Trisha O'Connell. She was thirty-two and had just started working as a study abroad advisor in Scranton's International Programs and Services office. She was beautiful and smart, with long strawberry blonde hair and signature red lipstick she never went anywhere without. After meeting at the new student convocation she and Jansson clicked instantly.

The two dated very happily the next two years, and Jansson could have continued to do so and be perfectly satisfied indefinitely. Then one night when they were discussing their future together, Trisha asked him his thoughts about getting married again, and he found himself balking.

With a great deal of difficulty, and knowing that what he was about to say would change everything for their relationship, he decided to be truthful and upfront.

"In all honesty…" he said, pausing for a long time before he was able to continue, "I don't know if I see myself every getting married again. To anyone. I just don't know if I've got it in me."

He looked into her eyes, which seemed as sad as he felt.

"I do love you, Trish."

"I know you do. I love you, too," she said, reaching for his hand and squeezing it tightly. "But I'm thirty four. I want to settle down and have a family. I need to be with a man who wants the same thing. I deserve someone who knows he wants to be with me for the rest of his life."

"You do deserve that. You don't know how much I wish I could be that for you."

With that, they decided to part ways. Jansson didn't want to say goodbye, but he knew it was unfair for her for them to continue the relationship if he was still unsure about the idea of marriage. Though painful, their split was amicable, and they were able to stay on friendly terms while still working at Scranton. Trisha now worked at the Center for International Education at William Patterson University in New Jersey and was married to a successful banker with whom she had two sons.

Jansson still got a Christmas card from them each year.

Jansson dated a few more women over the next few years, but formed no serious attachments. When Jansson was forty-six, he met a woman at the fiftieth birthday party of his friend Gabriel Arnaud. Her name was Charlotte Andrew and she was forty, owned a hugely successful event planning company, and was also divorced. She had dark brown hair, piercing blue eyes, and always dressed in the finest high-end clothing, clad in designer jewelry and handbags. She never left the house without being fully made up with the newest trending cosmetics from Chanel, Burberry, and Mark Jacobs. She was very business savvy, cultured, and sophisticated. Wanting to be as upfront as possible, Jansson had told Charlotte when they discussed getting serious that he was still unsure of his feelings about remarrying, and that although he couldn't promise her a ring, he could promise commitment and fidelity. At the time, Charlotte seemed to be alright with the situation.

Charlotte and Jansson dated very happily for almost a year and a half when their relationship began to unravel. It became clear that Charlotte had always intended on changing Jansson's mind about their future together. She appeared to bend over backward to appease him in every way, showering him with affection and expensive gifts. She was particularly determined to be as sexually adventurous with him as she was could, as though she thought it might make him forget she was over forty, which had never bothered Jansson to begin with. She started becoming vocally insecure about aging, and despite knowing Jansson's stance on marriage, started trying to pressure him into admitting it was a possibility.

Jansson tried to reason with her and make it clear that the subject of marriage was off the table, not merely because of his ambivalence on the subject, but also because Charlotte's behavior was starting to concern him. Even if he could see himself one day getting married to someone, he could see that that someone would definitely not be Charlotte. When she realized that marriage was a lost cause, Charlotte suggested instead that they try to have a baby. Jansson was flabbergasted at this proposal. He was also alarmed that her reaction to the marriage issue being shut down was to ask to have a baby.

"Having a baby is not a good idea," he told her, "Especially if we are not getting married. It's just not responsible. I already have a son, and I can't say I've been the greatest father to him."

Instead of letting the matter go, Charlotte continued to press Jansson on the baby issue. This quickly led Jansson to realize that the relationship was doomed and Charlotte's behavior bordered on the unstable. So with as much kindness and compassion as he could give, he told her the relationship could no longer continue.

Charlotte did not react well to being dumped. Weeks after Jansson broke things off with her, she called his phone, both home and work, constantly, leaving dozens of increasingly hysterical and pleading messages. When Jansson went to lunch one day with Gabriel Arnaud, at whose party he had met Charlotte, Gabriel told him that apparently Charlotte had been desperate to have children for many years. In fact, the reason that she and her ex-husband, Rich, split up was because she became so intensely focused on conceiving a child that she barely treated him as a husband and he felt more like a sperm donor than her spouse. Rich also wanted children, but after years of trying to get pregnant, he had wanted to start the process of adoption, something that Charlotte flatly refused to consider.

"You could have mentioned this to me when I told you we were dating!" Jansson had said to Gabriel incredulously.

"I only just found out myself," Gabriel had said. "Rich moved to Maine and cut himself off from their mutual friends for a while in order to distance himself from her. I only spoke to him in the past few weeks."

It turned out that Charlotte had been trying to get pregnant the whole time she and Jansson were together, telling him she had an IUD when in fact, she was using no birth control whatsoever. Jansson had no more contact with her after that, and last he'd heard, she had sold her business and moved to Fort Lauderdale where she was pursuing IVF and possible surrogacy. He wondered whether her dream of having a baby ever came true.

It was a combination of the ordeal with Charlotte and his horribly unsuccessful marriage to Margit that explained why Jansson, still a very eligible bachelor at age fifty-two, was still single. The truth was he had started to question everything after Margit's affair. The ease with which she had disposed of him, despite the fact that there had been no signs of marital discord before she left, baffled him. The two had been happily married (or so he thought) for nine years. Looking back on their marriage Jansson could see where the cracks had started to form.

When Jansson met Margit, he was twenty-six and she was twenty-two. He was going to school for his Swedish equivalent of a PhD while also working as a teaching assistant. She was lovely; stunning, in fact, with almost waist-length silvery blonde hair, electric-looking blue eyes and a complexion like a porcelain doll. She was passionate and vivacious and at the time was working as a clerk at a law office. She was very drawn to the tall, brooding, intellectual Alexander Jansson, with his steadfast dedication to academia and the future prospect of tenure at a major university in his not-too-distant future. During a trip to Jansson's grandmother's house one summer, Margit's ears had perked up when she overheard his mother and grandmother discussing money Jansson would eventually inherit from a great uncle. Eighteen months later they were married.

At the time Margit had thought of this future inheritance as an added bonus, for she did love him, and did not marry him for his financial prospects alone. At the start of their relationship she truly seemed to worship him. He was smart, handsome, steady, kind, and responsible. He took care of her. But she was selfish and impatient and eventually found herself becoming bored.

She realized she had grown tired of the predictability that came with being married; frustrated that Jansson wouldn't take her on more trips around Europe even though they had the means to do so. Jansson wanted to save for Gustaf's future. Margit wanted to use the money they had and show others that they had it. When Gustaf was a toddler, she found her eye wandering more frequently and she eventually gave into temptation with one of her coworkers, a striking Nils Asther look-alike. She would probably have stayed with Jansson for the financial stability and carried on her secret affair indefinitely had he not wanted to leave Sweden.

Jansson, for his part, knew his wife wasn't satisfied with how they handled money within their marriage. He knew there were aspects of their life together that she wasn't happy about, but they seemed to be superficial and no cause for worry. Their everyday life and interactions hadn't changed much so he went on thinking their relationship was still solid, even if Margit could be bratty about certain issues and when she didn't get her way. Her decision to leave and take Gustaf with her had so severely pulled the rug out from under him that he felt, even years later, his head was still spinning. He simply had not seen it coming. He found he was in no hurry to trust a woman in a relationship again.

He thought perhaps if he met the right person he could see being in a partnership with her for the rest of his life; and if she was, in fact, The One, eventually marrying her. But by now he was wary of looking for the right one, and because leaving his son a continent and an ocean away pained him so, he felt too guilty to ever want to have more children. He would never want Gustaf to feel like he had started a new family. He remained ambivalent about marriage, and at this point, he was still pretty gun-shy about dating. For the time being, friendship was just about all he could manage.

Neither Jansson nor Chelsea seemed to want to examine too closely the exact nature of their relationship. This was especially out of character for Jansson who was a responsible thinker, and had a tendency to overanalyze almost everything, courtesy of his psychology background and careful nature. It had been a long time since Jansson's last relationship, so he was quite used to spending his time alone. Not that he was in a relationship with Chelsea. It's just that it had been years since he had anyone to come home to after work or anything like a family waiting for him there each night.

Foothills was about forty-five minutes from Scranton, so Jansson commuted to work each day. He could have lived closer to the university, but he didn't want to live in Scranton itself. Scranton was a city to be sure, but not as Jansson knew cities. Being European and having traveled the continent, his idea of a metropolitan area was very different from Pennsylvanian standards. He was used to seeing the city lights reflecting off the Göta älv at night in his beloved Gothenburg, which was a major

Nordic port, and he decided if he couldn't reconcile the idea of city life in Pennsylvania, he would rather live in the country, further towards the mountains.

Because he commuted and spent so much time on the university campus, Jansson did not feel like he could ever have the company of a dog because of their need for constant companionship, to be taken on walks, and to run around outside. This disappointed Jansson, as he had always liked dogs, but he felt he could not give one a satisfactory home. So instead, the first year after he moved to Foothills, he went to a local shelter and adopted a cat. Cats usually looked after themselves and didn't need to be walked. They also weren't nearly as interactive or affectionate as dogs, but at least the ginger cat he had chosen was some company in his otherwise empty house.

As is typical of shelters, they had given the cat a name, Marmalade. Jansson found this name did not suit the animal in either gender or temperament. He christened his new pet Klaus. Klaus mostly kept to himself and since he was an outdoor cat during the day, would disappear for hours on end and generally live in his own world. He had one facial expression, a countenance that appeared to be of both boredom and distain. However, Jansson was glad to have him curled up on the couch while he graded papers or watched the news. Klaus was with him for seven years until one night he failed to come home. Jansson sadly concluded he must have been killed by a fox or the coyotes that were known to frequent the more rural parts of Foothills and its surrounding towns.

Because he had no one to come home to, when he was not working at the college he liked to spend his time doing research or getting involved with faculty advising. He enjoyed giving back his free time to the school. Supervising campus clubs and events kept him busy and improved his interaction with members of the university. Although he was used to his solitary routine, he certainly did not look forward to returning to an empty house each evening.

Having Chelsea around the house, enjoying dinner together, relaxing and watching television, or just talking, was a comfort for Jansson. If he had to assess their relationship with one another, he would say it was a friendship, but with a quality of a guardianship incorporated. He felt protective over her and somehow responsible for her welfare as he would for a favorite niece.

When Jansson told Chelsea about Klaus, she insisted the two go back to the shelter that weekend and pick out a new cat for him. Jansson was surprised that he had no objections to this, and wondered why he hadn't gotten another pet following Klaus's unfortunate disappearance.

They arrived at the shelter and picked a dark brown female tabby, not quite fully grown, with black markings and one white paw. She was quiet where most of the other cats were mewling ceaselessly. The name the shelter had given her was Oreo, ("This shelter certainly likes to name their animals after food," Jansson observed on the drive home.)

They brought her home and let her explore the house. While Jansson and Chelsea brainstormed a better name for his new pet, the cat revealed that she was not only quiet, she was also extremely skittish. She would walk several feet, freeze, arch her back, and then make a mad dash in the opposite direction and dive under the couch. Jansson eventually settled on the name Alice, as the creature was clearly lost in the Wonderland that was Jansson's farmhouse, and, as Chelsea pointed out, seemed to be somewhat chemically altered.

Chelsea also wondered about her friendship with Jansson. She felt a kinship with him, as though they had known each other for years rather than weeks. There was something familiar about his easy friendship, and in lieu of her own father, whom she knew she could not yet face, he was a very welcome surrogate parental figure.

The two had still not discussed the arrangement. It was as though they had reached an unspoken agreement; Chelsea was to stay there until further notice, no questions asked. She had asked him once if he wanted her to pay him rent but he refused and told her she was being silly.

"You're a guest here, not a tenant," he said.

She slept on the surprisingly comfortable pullout couch in his office. He had a guest bedroom, but had somehow managed to damage the futon he kept there for occasional guests when he tried to fold it back up into its couch shape. The wood had split in two, and given how infrequently he entertained overnight guests, he hadn't bothered to replace it. He offered to inflate an air mattress for Chelsea to put in the guest room so she would truly have her own space that wasn't his office, but Chelsea told him she preferred the pull-out to an air mattress and she didn't mind not technically being in a bedroom.

The situation felt almost as though she and Jansson were roommates (or in this case, housemates). Chelsea bought her own food at the grocery store, but often Jansson liked to make large dinners for the two of them on the weekends, so eventually they were sharing most of their food. It had been so long since Jansson had anyone to cook for, and he was happy to share his meals with Chelsea.

It was true that the dynamic between Chelsea and the professor was unconventional, but so far it seemed perfectly comfortable to them both, so neither thought much about what exactly was going on.

Try as she might, Chelsea found it very hard to ignore her growing feelings of curiosity about Jansson. She had an interest in him she could not identify. She could swear it wasn't a sexual or romantic interest, yet something about him was attractive to her. She tried not to dwell on it, but couldn't deny that it was there.

Though she didn't know exactly how old he was, she estimated that Jansson was somewhere around her father's age, maybe a bit older. This was a significant age gap between the two, yet he spoke to her like an adult, and they talked like old friends. Chelsea tried not to focus on the age difference between them because they got along so well, and it didn't seem to matter much.

She was curious about his past, which surprisingly hadn't come up in conversation very often. She wanted to know more about his family, his home country. She hadn't asked him whether he had ever been married or had any children or brothers or sisters. But she wondered about him. He was probably in his late-forties. He wasn't bad looking. He had nice blue eyes and was tall and burly, especially in his arms and shoulders. *It's not like he is a silver fox type*, Chelsea thought. *He doesn't even have gray hair.* True, he wasn't exactly George Clooney, but there were times she would look at him and find him handsome. She tried not to think like this, but she couldn't always control it.

One night she even dreamed about him. In the dream it was a cold winter's night, and she was locked out of the house. It was freezing and she was frightened. Jansson suddenly appeared, wrapped her in a blanket and lifted her just as easily as if she were made of feathers. He then carried her across the yard through glittering silver snowflakes, to where a white horse stood. The two of them mounted the horse and rode off into the night. She felt warm and safe with his arms wrapped snugly around her waist. She had awoken from the dream embarrassed, her face flushed. She tucked the dream in the back of her mind and tried to forget about it.

Still, there were times when she'd catch his eye and she'd feel a jerk, like her heart had suddenly dropped into her stomach. She could not explain why she felt this sensation because it was one she had always felt when she'd caught the eye of an attractive young man looking at her. Moments later the sensation would be gone and Chelsea would pretend it had never happened.

Jansson had nothing but tender feelings towards Chelsea. At first he convinced himself that the way he felt for her was like the feelings of a father. But after a while he could not deny his attraction to her, an attraction that was not fatherly in the least. Jansson of course, would never act on these feelings. It was wrong to take advantage of a girl in her situation. And she was so young, still finding her way, her future so uncertain. They came from different worlds, and were decades apart in life experience. The two of them could never work together, not in that way, at least. Jansson forced himself to quash any thoughts of possibility that something more than their current relationship would develop. If, by some crazy chance Chelsea reciprocated his feelings, he would let her decide how to handle the situation.

In the meantime, the days drifted into one another, and Chelsea found herself to be more at home with Jansson than she had ever felt when she lived with Greg.

Speaking of Greg, Chelsea found it quite surreal to be hiding out only one house over from him. She always waited until after he left for work to leave the Jansson's house, but she could easily see his comings and goings from the window in the living room. She found herself watching him as he went up and down the wooden stairs to the apartment. She could see when he left for work, when he had friends over (never any female friends though, curiously enough) and when he went out to the mailbox. During these times she would look him up and down and try to remember what it was she loved about him—or used to love about him— she wasn't sure which was true now. After a while she stopped watching him, her preoccupation with his daily routine growing less each day, and would only glance out the window to make sure the Subaru was gone, confirming he was not home.

She considered sending him a message saying that they were over, officially and unequivocally ending the relationship, maybe leaving it in the mailbox or sending him an email. But then she thought back to their final night together, that last fight, those last few weeks, and even months. The guy who had stopped caring, who had changed so much from the person she'd given her heart to, the one she left her family to share her life with...that man, the one she had fallen in love with, was gone. This was a different Greg altogether. The Greg who had hit her didn't deserve another word from her. Not one.

17

✴ ✴ ✴

I t was just before 4:30 p.m. Gene was the only
one working that afternoon at the tractor supply and repair shop and was hoping to close
up early. It had been a slow day. It was growing colder, and he wanted to get home and light a
fire in the fireplace. Fortunately the owner, his
friend A.J., treated Gene like a business partner and
let him make discretionary management decisions,
trusting him to close early on days when it became
clear business wasn't going to pick up. He had, after all, been working there almost twenty years.

He had sent Davis, the other mechanic, home
earlier than usual and locked up the garage. He
was just going over the credit card receipts and

double-checking the register when the bell on the door rang as someone entered.

Typical, thought Gene. There's always seemed to be that one jerk who insisted on coming in right before closing.

Gene didn't look up from the receipts immediately. Normally he would greet customers upon entry, but he just didn't feel much like going above and beyond the call of customer service duty that day.

When he saw in his peripheral vision that the customer was coming up to the counter he had no choice but to interact. He looked up and got a nasty shock when he saw that Greg was standing before him.

The two men silently sized one another up.

Not surprisingly, it was Gene who spoke first.

"I didn't think your tractor needed a tune-up until next season," he said coolly.

"I don't know if Chelsea's mentioned it to you, but I'm not much of a farmer," Greg said snidely.

Or much of an intellect, or a particularly valuable member of society, thought Gene. He looked the young man up and down. To Gene, Greg appeared to be the same as when he had last seen him: smug, careless, all muscle, and not quite at ease with his surroundings. He also didn't seem overly eager to explain his presence in the store given that he had no tractor.

"Then what can I help you with this afternoon, Greg?" Gene decided to dispense with any small talk. He'd had his fair share of chit-chatty tip-toeing around the true issue nonsense from Patrick Frye, and he was not interested in beating around whatever weird bush Greg had brought into the store.

"I was wondering if you wouldn't mind asking Chelsea to return my calls."

Return his calls.

Why would she need to call him if they lived in the same apartment?

Gene quickly concluded that Chelsea wasn't living with Greg anymore, at least not for the moment. Did Greg think that Chelsea was back at home with Gene? Gene wasn't sure what was going on, but he sure as hell wasn't about to admit to Greg that he knew nothing about Chelsea's current whereabouts.

"I don't really feel comfortable getting in the middle of whatever it is that's going on between the two of you," he said, noncommittally.

"Come on, it's not getting in the middle to just have her answer her phone for once," Greg said.

Gene could tell Greg was trying to play nice but wasn't very good at it, struggling to mask his impatience. Greg wasn't used to having to be polite to others. Mostly he got what he wanted by turning on the charm extra thick. Normally his ability to sweet-talk coupled with a winning smile served him well and he only ever needed to use flattery to achieve his means. He would never lower himself to sucking up. While many who knew Greg found him quite charming, Gene had always considered his air to be smarmy, his attitude smug, and his manners lacking. Perhaps this why was neither of Chelsea's parents had been taken in by Greg's charismatic ways.

"Well, you know Chelsea," Gene said with a small smile, "She does things in her own way, in her own time."

He never thought he would appreciate using this particular argument because it was such a source of his own chagrin, but he had to admit, he was enjoying frustrating Greg's efforts.

"Just tell her to give me some sign that she's not lying in a ditch somewhere. Last time I checked, girlfriends weren't supposed to go weeks without talking to their man."

Weeks without talking to their man.

Gene tried to keep his face inscrutable. This meant Chelsea had been not living with Greg for a while now. Gene had been excited at first, but now his brain started to explore the possibility that his daughter may in fact be lying in a ditch some-where. He started to feel very uneasy. He couldn't remember how long it had been since the last time he talked to her on the phone.

When Gene didn't say anything for a moment, Greg pressed further.

"Did you know she's not even going to work anymore either? Her manager says he took her off the schedule."

"She's got her reasons," Gene said, trying to act as though he knew details Greg did not.

"Yeah, like she's sick of actually working and she wants to go back to school and have you pay for everything," Greg said, cocking an eyebrow.

You little shit, thought Gene. He could tell Greg was intentionally baiting him.

"Greg, I'm sure she'll call you when she feels like talking," Gene said, trying to emphasize the finality in his voice. He was done dealing with Greg. He'd had enough for one afternoon and for a lifetime.

"But..."

"I'm sorry, my friend; but we're actually clos-ing up shop early today, so I'll have to say goodbye for the afternoon."

In five seconds flat, Gene came around the counter and gently but firmly ushered Greg out the door, locked it behind him, and placidly turned the sign on the door so it read "Closed".

Then he went directly for his phone. Chelsea had some explaining to do.

CR

Chelsea was browsing the Internet on Jansson's computer. She was half-heartedly researching some of the classes Jansson had recommended to her on the University of Scranton website. Not that she was interested in college courses, she told herself. This research was purely for curiosity's sake. She would delete the browsing history when she was done.

She heard her cell phone ringing. Chelsea glanced at the phone's screen to see who was calling. She didn't feel much like talking to anyone but if it was one of her girlfriends she'd consider answering it. But the words lighting up as her phone buzzed were "DAD CELL".

It was her father calling.

Her dad rarely called her. He usually waited for her to make contact with him. She figured he did this because he'd learned she didn't appreciate any suggestion that he was trying to interfere in her life. She knew her dad well enough to recognize when he was trying to avoid confrontation. She stared at the phone as it rang twice, then three times. She remembered she hadn't spoken to him since she left Greg which was weeks ago. She realized he must be getting worried. Chelsea sat motionless until the phone stopped ringing. She didn't know why, but she was too nervous to answer her father's call. She was certainly not ready to explain what was going on.

A few moments later her phone buzzed again signaling that she had a new voicemail. She took a deep breath, opened her phone and dialed her inbox.

"Hi Chels, it's Dad..." the message said, "I'm just calling you because Greg stopped into the store today looking for you. He says you haven't been living with him for the past couple weeks and he can't get a hold of you and doesn't know where you are. Please call me and let me know you're alright. As soon as you can, Chels."

She thought for a minute. There had been tension between her and her father because of Greg for a long time. She loved her dad, but for so long her loyalty had been to her boyfriend, and she remembered feeling judged and misunderstood by her parents about her relationship with Greg and her decision to not go to college. But all that didn't seem to matter now. In fact, the more she thought about it, the more she realized her relationship with Greg was the only real source of estrangement between herself and her father. She had chosen Greg over her family, over school, over an education. She had chosen Greg over her sick mother. The reason she hadn't spoken to her father since the night she ran away from Greg was because she was ashamed. She had been wrong and now she could see it clearly. She had been telling her parents that she was an adult and could make her own decisions—who she dated, how she lived her life, whether or not she wanted to go to college—she had been adamant that they were wrong to judge her, and had no right to interfere.

But it turned out they had been right about Greg all along. Marybeth told Chelsea he was irresponsible, that he wasn't going to change. Both her parents warned her that he was a bad influence and that he had too much sway on Chelsea's life choices. She had resented them. She was sure she was making choices based on what she wanted, independent from Greg's influence. But look where it had gotten her. Homeless, jobless, hiding out in a neighbor's house and hit across the face.

Shit, she thought, *Mom and Dad were right. Danielle was right. How could I have been so damn stupid?* Self-awareness, she discovered, was terribly inconvenient. *When you are self-aware*, she thought, *you have to hold yourself accountable for all the crap you've done, even if you're still too ashamed.*

She waited for a few minutes. She had to make sure she was ready for this call. Finally she picked up her phone. Even if she wasn't ready to go home, to own up to all the mistakes she had made, she should at least tell her dad she was alright and was staying somewhere safe. As she began dialing her home number, her heart began to beat faster, and her stomach felt somewhat queasy. Feeling nervous surprised her.

Calm down, she instructed herself. *This is my dad.*

She hit the send button and waited. The phone rang twice…three times…

Finally, he picked up.

"Hello?"

"Hi Dad, it's Chelsea." She waited for a response. She heard him exhale a sigh of relief.

Gene wasted no time getting down to business.

"Why is Greg coming to my job looking for you? Where are you staying if you're not living in his apartment with him?" Gene sounded stern, like he was demanding an explanation, but Chelsea could hear the concern in his voice. She knew he was pleading for answers from her, hoping that this meant she would be coming home and wondering why she hadn't yet.

"We had a huge fight a couple of weeks ago," Chelsea began. She took a deep breath and changed the phone to her other ear. She realized her palms were sweaty. She wiped them on her jeans, forcing herself to continue her explanation. "He was drunk and all strung out and it was just the last straw. So I moved out and didn't tell him where. I'm staying at a friend's house for now, while I work out what I'm going to do."

She decided to leave the fact that she was living with a male professor in his fifties out of it. Telling him she was staying with "a friend" was technically the truth. Let him think that she was staying with a girlfriend, he wouldn't worry. She hoped this explanation would be enough to assure her father that Greg was out of her life, so he wouldn't press her on the subject since it was not in his nature to pry. But Gene wasn't going to let Chelsea off the hook so easily. Not this time.

"But he says he tried going to your work. He says your manager doesn't have you on the schedule anymore and he thinks you haven't been going."

She felt a pang in her chest. Greg had been looking for her at the Mountain Range Grille?

"I've been kind of lying low for a while. I think I may have mono so I've been working fewer shifts." She decided to stick to the story she had asked Brooke to tell their manager.

"When he showed up, I wasn't sure whether you'd left him or if something had happened to you." His tone sounded neutral but she was positive he was mightily unhappy about hearing that his daughter was untraceable from the boyfriend that he'd always hated.

She swallowed hard. She should have thought about that.

"I know, Dad. I'm sorry. I just got so overwhelmed with moving out of the apartment and trying to figure out what to do next that I didn't realize how it looked. I'm surprised Greg even cares. I took most of my stuff out of his place while he was gone. You'd think he'd have noticed."

"He knows you left him, kid. I just don't think he knows it's over."

"Well it is over," she said firmly, filled with satisfaction that she'd not only said it, but that now she truly believed it. It was over. No more Greg. That chapter of her life was closed.

There was silence on the other end of the line, and while she couldn't see his face, she felt sure there was triumph her dad's eyes.

"Anyway," she continued "I just need some time to work stuff out. But I'm sorry he ambushed you like that. I didn't mean to worry you. I should have let you know sooner."

"Do you need anything? Money? If you're working fewer shifts…"

"I'm okay, Dad. Really. I have some savings, and as soon as I'm feeling better I'll be back to a full work week. You don't have to worry."

"Okay…" he said, sounding doubtful. He paused, then said, "You know you can always come home." He tried to sound casual but Chelsea could hear the hopefulness in his voice.

"I know. I'll let you know once I've figured everything out. I'll keep it touch, Dad. I promise."

He sighed deeply, and Chelsea knew he wasn't sure if he could believe her promise.

"Alright, Chelsea. Thanks for calling."

"Bye, Dad."

Chelsea closed her phone. She had no idea what her next move would be.

18

★ ★ ★

Jansson arrived home early that Friday evening. He came through the door as Chelsea was perusing the kitchen trying to figure out what she wanted to make for dinner.

"Tonight, we celebrate," he announced, grinning widely. "I received some very good news this afternoon."

"What are we celebrating?"

"The head of the psychology department announced over the summer that he would be retiring at the end of this academic year. It's official. You're looking at the future head of the psychology department."

Jansson had known for a while he was a top contender for the position of department head, but there was another professor, a tenured social psychology instructor whom Jansson considered to be totally unapproachable, especially to students, who was also vying for the title. In the end Jansson easily came out on top, especially given his dedication to the department and student achievement. The dean called him that afternoon to give him the official word. After sending Gustaf an email sharing his good news, Jansson rushed home to share it with Chelsea.

"I don't know about you, but I think tonight calls for dining out. What do you think?"

Chelsea beamed back at Jansson who seemed to be lit up with pride.

"That sounds perfect. Where shall we go?"

Jansson picked out a nice steak and seafood restaurant where the two of them enjoyed a very pleasant meal. Chelsea ordered the lobster alfredo and Jansson ordered a New York strip steak. They also ordered dessert; Chelsea picked the Oreo cheesecake and Jansson picked the raspberry torte.

When they returned from dinner, Jansson was still feeling jubilant and wanted to continue to celebrate. He brought out a fancy bottle of merlot he'd gotten as a gift months before and had not had occasion to open it until now. He poured himself a glass. Chelsea reached for a wine glass of her own and placed it beside Jansson's. He looked at it uncertainly and then poured only a tiny splash into the glass.

"That's it?" she laughed.

Jansson raised his eyebrows. He didn't pour her anymore.

"It's not a good idea to give someone too much wine when she isn't twenty-one yet."

Chelsea rolled her eyes.

"Then pretend we're back in Sweden. I'd be able to legally drink there. And it's not like I don't drink now."

"Yes, I know how you young people feel about the drinking age here and how much attention you pay it," said Jansson. He put the bottle down, cementing his refusal to give her any more wine. She took the bottle and generously filled her own glass.

"Don't say I didn't warn you," Jansson half-laughed, but then looked apprehensive, as though he was doing something to enable delinquency.

"It'll be fine, don't worry," Chelsea said.

Jansson gave a small laugh and shook his head. "Famous last words, my dear," he said.

The two had a good time drinking the wine, talking, and laughing together. Chelsea voiced something that had been on her mind for some time. "So I've been wondering...I once found a letter to you in my mailbox and had to bring it over to your house. How come it wasn't addressed to *Doctor* Jansson? Don't most professors have PhDs?"

Jansson replied, "The doctoral degree here is different than in Sweden and in Europe. It's complicated. I have the Swedish equivalent of an American PhD but we study for different lengths of time for each degree and we take different licensing tests."

"Doesn't that make studying abroad more complicated? I mean with all the differences in degrees?" Chelsea said, pouring herself another glass.

"I guess it depends. Each school is different about how it accepts and transfers credits. I did my bachelor's work abroad in Scotland but then did all my post-grad work back home in Sweden and was able to get my licentiate without any problems. It works out. Plenty of students study abroad in Europe."

Chelsea was starting to think that missing out on the chance to study abroad was a decent enough incentive to reconsider passing up college. Everything Jansson had told her about Sweden, Scotland, and the handful of other countries in Europe he had visited made her eager to travel and see foreign cities for herself.

Before they knew it, the bottle was nearly empty. It wasn't a small bottle, either, and truth be told, Chelsea was doing the majority of the drinking.

With each glass she finished, she then refilled another. They were sitting in the living room but Chelsea abruptly stood up. Then she swayed slightly.

"I...need to lie down," she laughed. She made her way towards the office, where she usually slept on the pull-out couch, but at the last moment turned and started to clumsily make her way up the stairs, half walking, half crawling at times. Jansson hesitated, and then followed her. She had made her way tipsily into Jansson's bedroom and collapsed onto the bed.

Jansson hovered at the door for a moment. With much reservation, he moved into the room. Chelsea curled onto her side as she sank into the soft mattress. Jansson felt his head start to get lighter, so he sat on the bed, but on the opposite side of Chelsea, in the farthest corner, and completely upright.

"They should put a warning on that merlot, it sneaks up on you," he said with a small shake of his head.

"I never used to be such a lightweight," she said rolling onto her other side to face him and laughing unconcernedly.

Cautiously, Jansson eased back onto the mattress, but far away from where Chelsea was sprawled out. They both lay there in silence for a moment. Chelsea's head was swimming. It had been a long time since she'd had any alcohol, and on the nights she used to join Greg while he drank, their beverage of choice was usually beer. Now the red wine was hitting her swift and hard. She had already experienced that moment of awareness in which she acknowledged inwardly that she was drunk, but she didn't tell Jansson. Instead she just let the happy sensation flow throughout her body, not caring, for the first time in weeks, about anything.

Jansson was tired. He buried his face in one of the pillows. He felt as though he was in a dream, simultaneously awake and asleep. He was aware of the soft heaviness of the pillow, the warmth of the down comforter, Chelsea lying next to him. Jansson was not usually one to get drunk. He typically only drank in social situations and couldn't remember drinking for the express purpose of getting drunk since his college years with his friends back in Sweden. In fact, he wasn't drunk at the moment. But he wasn't exactly stone cold sober either.

At that moment he felt slightly dizzy, as though the bed itself were spinning and he and Chelsea were whirling around the room. His arm brushed some part of her body, but he couldn't tell which part. It didn't matter, her hair, her hand, her face. Chelsea could hear Jansson's slow steady breathing. She could feel his inhales and exhales through the mattress. It was a comforting sound. When she went to stretch one of her legs away from her she brushed against his leg and for a brief moment his breathing halted, before returning back to normal.

They lay together, not speaking, but in that silence there was a great deal going on. As they swayed from the wine, both of them feeling warm and flushed, they tossed and turned on the bed as one does when having difficulty sleeping. Finally Jansson's large, gentle hand found the small of Chelsea's back. And in the darkness, between the motions, the unspoken understanding, and the light touching of skin to skin, Chelsea and Jansson disappeared under the blankets.

Chelsea awoke with a start. She felt her head pounding. She had been hungover before, and recognized the familiar deep aching in her skull. She realized she was not lying on the pull-out couch in Jansson's study where she usually slept. She was wearing only a cami and panties.

Her head swam. What had she done last night?

She rolled over slowly and saw Jansson sleeping next to her. The clock on the nightstand next to his bed blared red and hurt her eyes: 6:09 a.m. She quietly got out of bed, so as not to wake Jansson, and picked up her jeans from the floor, along with her bra and her sweater. She crept downstairs, into the office, and pulled the sliding door shut. She climbed into the pull-out couch and wrapped the afghan around her. Before she should think or worry about what happened between her and Jansson, her pounding head pulled her back to sleep.

Jansson woke up almost an hour later, acutely aware of the fact that Chelsea had spent the night in his bed. After a moment he realized she was no longer sleeping next to him. Unlike Chelsea, he remembered everything that happened the previous night. He pulled his pillow over his face. How could he have let anything happen? He felt ashamed at the memory of the happiness he had felt while he had held her.

Suddenly he sat up.

What if she was gone? What if she had awoken next to him that morning and been so horrified that she had taken her things and left?

As quietly as he could, he pulled on his robe, and quickly walked downstairs and down the hall to the office door. He opened it a crack, and saw with relief that she was fast asleep on the pullout couch.

He then immediately started busying himself with making breakfast. He pulled out everything he had in his house; eggs, bacon, toast, sausage, and began cooking in a frenzy. They would have to talk about it. There was no way around it; they could not go back and pretend last night had not happened. He did not know what it meant, but he hoped that whatever friendship between them had not been completely destroyed by one drunken act.

Jansson could have kicked himself. This was exactly what he didn't want. For her to feel like he had taken advantage, that he had brought her into his home for anything other than her own safety and well-being. He himself had not wanted to feel like he had taken advantage of her. His mind flashed back to the events of last night. He cursed himself for not being more careful and in control of the situation.

Chelsea woke up to the smell of breakfast and the sound of Jansson moving around the kitchen. He was not usually this loud in the mornings. Maybe he was intentionally trying to wake her with the sound of cooking, or maybe it was her hangover amplifying the clanging sounds of pots and pans. Her head still hurt and her tongue felt dry, but her mind was clearer now. She was remembering bits and pieces of the previous night. She remembered going out to eat, coming back to the house and drinking the wine...Jansson's bed...Jansson. She was pretty sure she knew what had happened, that she hadn't dreamed it. But it was not something she wanted to discuss. Not now, anyway. She pulled on some sweats and shuffled out into the kitchen where Jansson looked very much occupied with his breakfast-making.

He was bustling around moving pans and opening drawers, tending to multiple things at once, so focused that he didn't hear her come into the room.

"Good morning," she said trying to sound casual and groggy.

Jansson looked up from his cooking.

"Good morning, Chelsea," he said, sounding oddly formal. He went back to his bustling.

She wanted to say something else, but she couldn't think of anything. She didn't like feeling as though he was intentionally avoiding her gaze.

Finally she threw caution to the wind and said, "Everything smells so great, I'm glad you're making hangover food."

It was an indirect acknowledgment of the night before.

Jansson hesitated then said, "Yes I thought a big breakfast and some greasy food was in order after too much wine."

"Can I help with anything?" Chelsea asked.

"If you just want to get some bread out and put it in the toaster," he suggested. He was still not really meeting her eyes.

The two moved around the kitchen without speaking for a few minutes. Then they finally sat down at the table.

"It looks good," she said.

"Thank you, I hope you enjoy it," Jansson returned.

There was a brief silence while they began to eat and then Chelsea said "Next time we should just stick to champagne."

Jansson looked up. She was smiling tentatively. He smiled back. They were not going to discuss it, not today, maybe not ever.

"Yes, definitely…" he said "Next time."

He was safe for another day.

19

★ ★ ★

Two weeks later, Chelsea set out for her daily walk earlier than usual. Taking long walks had become part of her routine, but normally she went after lunch instead of mid-morning. Today she felt like getting an early start. She waited until after Greg's car pulled out of the driveway next door as he headed to work the way she did each day before she dared to leave Jansson's house.

The temperature was dropping now that autumn was in full swing. Chelsea pulled on a hoodie and then her charcoal-colored peacoat, something Greg bought her for Christmas the year before, and stepped out into the chilly air. She needed to think about her plans for the future, both immediate and long-term, and her lengthy walks were the perfect time to get in some quality thinking time. She had a lot to consider. She needed to go back to work soon. She had been smart about saving her money, and had a little savings in her account at the bank that she was using to pay for groceries and her phone bill, but she knew she needed to go back to the restaurant if she was eventually going to be able to pay rent for her own apartment.

She turned onto a street with a steep hill, picking up her pace a bit. She liked walking. As a server she was used to being on her feet for several hours at a time, and she was glad to be keeping active even though she hadn't worked a shift in weeks. She enjoyed the crunching sound of the fallen leaves beneath her feet and the brightly colored trees all around her. She thought for a moment that she could now understand her father's appreciation for nature. She felt completely at ease. She loved the smell of autumn. She inhaled the aroma of the leaves, the smoke from a distant wood-burning stove, and the brisk air. Fall meant pumpkin spice-flavored beverages, apple pies, jack-o-lantern carving, and stylish, warm clothing.

She walked for about an hour and then headed back towards the farmhouse. She thought dreamily about how the time was passing, about how life with Jansson was so comfortable, away from Greg and without having to worry about going into work, not having to write down her schedule, which technically was supposed to stay the same from week to week, but the servers always swapped shifts which would often disrupt her set schedule. She was glad to not have to worry about which days she had swapped and which days she was working. It had made her lose track of the date, the day of the week, each day sliding easily into the next.

Her next thought hit her like a ton of bricks. She felt like her heart was plummeting from her chest faster than the elevator on the Tower of Terror ride at Disneyworld where the Shepherds had taken a family vacation when she was eleven. Her brain felt fuzzy and she couldn't think what day it was, what month, and she realized with a horrible sensation as though she'd been punched in the stomach that she had no idea when her last period was.

Her breath caught in her chest, and she could feel the cold air searing the sides of her throat. She pulled out her phone and found its mini-calendar tool. She looked through the days, hoping for anything that would jog her memory as to when she was supposed to have started her period. But the numbers were no help. They looked foreign, as though she were looking at a different language.

Think, Chelsea, she ordered herself, *Concentrate!*

Then she remembered the one crucial item she hadn't grabbed when she and Brooke broke into the apartment that day: her birth control pills. She knew exactly where they were, she could picture them now. They were in the drawer on the side table next to the bed. All those pills in that round pink container just next door. And at that moment she knew it must be weeks past when her time of the month was supposed to have started. She quickened her pace, wanting to get back to Jansson's house as soon as possible. She felt hot and sick, her mind reeling as she started to sweat despite the cool temperature of the day.

"Shit, shit, shit!" she muttered to herself as she pulled out the key Jansson had given her. It was true that when she ran from the apartment the night Greg hit her, she had more pressing matters on her mind than birth control; her safety, for instance. Then after she left Greg, she had so much on her plate that the subject of sex wasn't even on her radar.

But there was that one night, she thought, *that one night in Jansson's bed.* They had both been drinking. She had been drunk. Something had happened. She also realized with growing panic that two nights before she ran away from Greg's apartment the two of them had slept together and that the pill she took that night was the last pill she had taken since.

Oh God, oh God, this can't be happening to me...

Chelsea didn't know what she was expecting to do once she was back in the house. She still felt like she was frantically treading water. She made a strenuous effort to quell her rising panic. It was warmer in the house and she could sit down to think. She could calm down and be rational. No, she hadn't gotten her period. But she was under extreme stress from everything that was going on in her life; what happened with Greg, not having a job. She also had no symptoms of early pregnancy. She did not feel nauseous, lightheaded or even tired, her breasts did not hurt. Her missing period was her only real cause for concern. But periods were late all the time. Any number of factors could cause someone's cycle to be thrown off.

Still, Chelsea had to know for sure.

Although she felt like her whole body was shaking, she reached for the phone with a steady hand, and dialed a number she knew well.

"How much do I owe you?" Chelsea asked the instant Brooke walked in the door with the pharmacy bag in her hand.

"Twelve dollars," Brooke said, setting the bag on Jansson's coffee table and taking off her coat. Instead of handing the purchase to Chelsea, she appeared to be making herself comfortable on the couch.

"Now what is all this about. You think you're having Greg's kid?"

Chelsea tried to sit with Brooke on the couch but she was too antsy. She sat down then stood up again, nervously wringing her hands, twirling her hair or tugging on the bottom of her blouse.

"I don't know. I could be. I forgot to grab my birth control when we broke into the apartment that day. And Greg and I had sex the last week I stayed there...two nights before I left."

Brooke watched as Chelsea paced back and forth. She knew exactly how Chelsea was feeling. She had been twitchy and anxious before she knew for sure she was pregnant with Quinn.

"Yeah, but it's not like you've had sex since then."

Chelsea stopped pacing and stared at Brooke. She looked like a deer caught in the headlights.

"Or have you and the professor been doing some extracurricular activities?" Brooke was blunt.

No beating around the bush, no bullshit, just straight to the point. It was very difficult to get anything past Brooke.

"We haven't been," Chelsea cleared her throat, "I mean we aren't sleeping together, it's not that kind of thing."

Brooke raised her eyebrows. "But...?"

Chelsea looked uncomfortable and started tugging at the ends of her hair again.

"But there was this one night. I can't remember exactly what happened... we shared a bottle of wine because he found out he kind of got a promotion. I got drunk. I'm pretty sure something happened, I think I remember it happening." She paused. "I know *something happened.* I woke up in his bed half naked. I don't know exactly how far things went."

And then Brooke voiced Chelsea's other biggest concern, besides whether or not she was pregnant. The last thing she needed now was to qualify as a guest star on a paternity test episode of *The Maury Show*.

"So it could be Greg's, or it could be his," Brooke said matter-of-factly.

"Or it could be neither! I might not be pregnant at all, there's more than one reason for a woman to stop getting her period. I could be sick, or stressed."

Brooke saw the look of barely controlled panic in her friend's face. It was unlike Chelsea to be so undone. Normally Chelsea was very together and composed. Brooke took a deep breath. There was no reason to jump to conclusions. It was best to keep calm.

"Well," Brooke said reaching towards the brown paper bag, "that's what this test is for."

Chelsea blanched. The test.

"Oh God Brooke, what'll I do if…"

"You'll figure something out. Let's not worry before we have to. Go get some water or juice from the kitchen, then come back here," she told Chelsea.

"What? Why?"

"Because you need to have something in your bladder for this to work. A full bladder is best. Now go get something to drink."

Chelsea went to the kitchen and returned a minute later with a full glass of water. She tried to chug the whole thing at once so she could take the test as soon as possible. But as she tried to down the whole glass, found that the iron fist that seemed to have taken hold of her chest since she realized she could be pregnant wouldn't let her do any more than take small sips at a time. She tried to relax. Hyperventilating would not help the situation.

"When I took my first pregnancy test, I was so scared that my body wouldn't let me pee even though I felt like I was about to explode," Brooke said. She left out the fact that the first time she took that test was when she was only fourteen years old.

Chelsea smiled weakly. She wouldn't be surprised if her body did the same thing. She felt almost paralyzed with anxiety, so how was her body supposed to function normally?

She was grateful for one thing; Jansson mentioned he had a meeting after his last class that day, so he wouldn't be home until at least seven or eight. She and Brooke had time.

Brooke made Chelsea drink three large glasses of water and encouraged her to try and eat a bagel.

"It sometimes helps if you have something in your stomach," she explained.

Chelsea could only pick at the bagel. She managed three or four big bites before pushing it away. She couldn't stomach any more.

Finally when Chelsea felt like her bladder was about to burst, Brooke instructed her to go to the bathroom. When she came out, all they could do was wait the three minutes it would take for results to show up.

Chelsea was nauseous, but was sure that it was from nerves, not morning sickness. The two of them sat in silence. Brooke knew it would do Chelsea no good to pretend to gossip or take her mind off the timer she'd set on her cell phone.

After the longest three minutes of her life, Chelsea felt her phone buzz as the alarm when off. She had set the pregnancy test on a napkin on the coffee table, just out of her reach and turned away so she couldn't catch a glimpse before she was ready.

"Do you want me to tell you?" Brooke offered.

"No, I need to look myself," said Chelsea.

Grow up, Chelsea she ordered herself. *Look at the test. You wanted to be an adult, now you have to deal with adult issues. Look at the test. Look now.*

She reached over and grabbed the test, and simultaneously she caught a glimpse of the pink symbol that had appeared.

She stared at the plastic stick in her hands. She felt like the floor was falling from beneath her. There in front of her was an unmistakable solid pink plus-sign. Positive. Pregnant. She inhaled deeply and when she exhaled all the fear and anxiety that had taken hold over her body since her walk earlier that day flowed out of her. She felt Brooke move from the couch to the loveseat next to her. Brooke squeezed her shoulder and didn't say anything, letting Chelsea sit and absorb.

Chelsea knew she should feel panic, fear, even shame that she hadn't been more careful. But she didn't. She was numb, and she knew all those feelings would come soon enough. For now she couldn't think about what that positive test meant, what she would do about it, who, if anyone, she would tell. For now she was content in her numbness.

☙

She sat on the couch in the living room staring into space. Alice the cat sat beside her, twitching at the sound of the wind outside or the heat moving through the pipes of the old farmhouse, quivering at some unknown threat. Brooke had left a few minutes before, but promised to stop by the next day to see how Chelsea was doing. Chelsea needed time to process the situation. She sat in silence for a long time. She tried to pet Alice, but the cat sprang off the couch and tore up the stairs when Chelsea reached for her.

Jansson had a stereo in the living room. Slowly Chelsea stood up and walked over to it. She flipped on the radio. She needed something else in her head besides the symbol she had just seen on the stick. She closed her eyes and listened to the music. After scanning stations for a while, she found one playing the song *Man in the Mirror*. It made her think of dance class. Her former dance instructor, Jeanine, always loved playing Michael Jackson songs for the girls to dance free-style and warm up to before class.

In that moment she truly missed dancing. She thought longingly of the freeing feeling of the motion and rhythm she knew so well from all her years of dance classes and performance. She doubted she was even remotely as flexible and strong as she used to be. She longed for her days in the dance studio with her friends in the advanced classes, dancing her heart out, back when she was still a child...before her mother had been diagnosed with cancer...before she was grown up...before she had anything to worry about but her lines and pointed toes...before Greg, and employment, and pregnancy tests, before she had any real problems or cares, when she could simply be.

She stood up. She remembered being a little girl in her pink sparkly tutu her mother had sewn for her. She started to sway with the music. Bon Jovi's *It's My Life* was now playing. She turned the volume dial as far up as it went. She shut her eyes tight and started to move around the room, her muscle memory slowly returning to her, finding her natural inclination to dance was just as it always had been. Then she started to spin, around and around, losing all sense of time and space, not caring which way was up, which was down, what had happened in the past or what lay in store for her in the future. She simply spun and spun to the music, starting to get dizzy but she didn't stop.

She twirled and danced and realized in that instant she wished she could be a little girl again, the girl she was when she was younger; her mother and father's Mexican Jumping Bean. She wanted to go back to the time when she didn't have to think about anything but the feeling of the twirling around the room, completely immersed in the music.

She heard Jon Bon Jovi's distinct voice croon over the radio in a song about yearning to *live* while he was alive.

If only, Chelsea thought. *If only...*

Part III

20

Chelsea didn't tell anyone that she was pregnant. She certainly couldn't bring herself to tell Jansson. She couldn't imagine what she would say, let alone how she would deal with the possibility that it was his child. She still wasn't even sure if they really had slept together or if things had stopped before it went that far. She had to decide how she was going to handle the situation before she told anyone besides Brooke.

Despite everything that had happened and her carefully kept secret, she and Jansson remained remarkably normal in their interactions. They continued their days as though the drunken night had never happened, and they still had dinner, watched movies, talked, and sat together just as they did before. Except now, Chelsea couldn't pretend that time had stopped just for her. She had to admit that she needed to straighten out her life, and soon. It wasn't just her own life she had to consider. There was going to be a baby. She had to consider her child as well as herself. Her future weighed heavily on her mind, and while she wanted to enjoy her time with Jansson, she knew it couldn't last much longer.

One night she was in the kitchen making brownies from a box mix, every so often checking them in the oven with a toothpick. Jansson sat at the kitchen table, pouring over the *New York Times*. He seemed especially quiet that evening.

Seemingly out of the blue, he turned his head to Chelsea and said, "I just want you to know how I've enjoyed having you here."

Chelsea turned to face him. She wasn't sure where he was going with this. It sounded almost as though he was trying to say goodbye.

"I can't even begin to thank you for taking me in," Chelsea said.

Jansson eyes seemed to smile at her, though his mouth remained slack.

"You don't need to, Chelsea. You and I have become good friends. We must have fallen into each other's lives for a reason. And for once I don't feel the need to analyze it. I just wanted to let you know that having someone here, a friend, has really done me a great deal of good."

Chelsea was quiet for a minute.

"I think it's been good for me, too. And it's more than just having a place to live. It's about having..." she paused, not sure how to word what she was feeling, "...someone." she decided.

"I know," he replied. "Believe me, I know."

Chelsea looked up at Jansson, and then voiced for the first time something that had been on her mind since the night she appeared on his doorstep.

"Alexander. Alexander was my brother's name," she said.

"I thought you said you were an only child," said Jansson.

"Well, I had a brother once. He died when he was born. Or before that. He was stillborn. I never even saw him. Sometimes I wonder what my life would be like if he had lived and we'd grown up together."

Without realizing what she was doing, she ran her hand over her middle, pausing briefly over the spot where her baby was growing. When she realized what her hand was doing she quickly removed it. Fortunately Jansson seemed not to have noticed the gesture. They were both silent for moment.

"I lost a little boy once, too," said Jansson. His voice was gentle, empathetic, but strangely distant. Chelsea scrutinized him. His chin was resting on his folded hands, as he gazed placidly out the glass of his porch door into the moonlight.

Chelsea's breath caught in her chest.

"He died?"

"Oh no," said Jansson, "My son is alive and well, thank goodness. I've mentioned him before, my son, Gustaf. He's actually in his third year at Oxford."

Chelsea shook her head, but said nothing. She was confused but knew he would continue to explain without her prompting. She recalled that Jansson spoken of having a son in the weeks since she had been living with him, but he did so in a way that made it clear there was some estrangement between them, so Chelsea had never pursued the subject.

"My ex-wife took him with her when she left me. He was only six." The pale blue light of the evening shone over Jansson's face. He was still gazing out the window.

"After they moved out of the house, Margit told Gustaf that I was the one who didn't want to be a family anymore and that I cared more about teaching students in America than being a father and husband. Gustaf was too young to understand, really, but he did know that I wasn't around anymore and that the man Margit left me for was the one who was around. Between the two of them they filled Gustaf's head with enough lies about me that I had little hope of ever having a real relationship with him." He paused, and then added, "Being a continent away doesn't help the situation either."

Jansson now looked about as uncomfortable as Chelsea had ever seen him.

Chelsea took in this information. It all seemed so heavy. There was still so much she didn't know about Jansson, and hearing him now speak about how his son grew up without him seemed to not fit with the man she had been living with and befriended. It seemed rather incongruous that someone who had been so kind to her, even before they had really met, had so much distance between himself and his son.

At last she spoke.

"Couldn't you have hired a lawyer? I mean, couldn't you have fought your ex-wife for custody and told your son the truth?"

She tried to keep her voice impassive. She didn't want to judge him, as he did not judge her, and she certainly wasn't winning any awards herself for how to treat your family. Still, she really wanted to hear that Jansson was just as good to his son as he had been to her. She wanted to keep thinking of him in the same way she always had, with his kindness and steadiness. She didn't think she could accept that he might be like her, and everyone else: flawed and fucked up.

Alice the cat padded into the kitchen toward her food dish, paused near Jansson's leg, and then, as though sensing this was a serious conversation, or else just being her usual weird self, suddenly sprinted off into the office.

"I hired an attorney who got me two months with Gustaf a year. I returned to my mother's house in Sweden from June to August each year and I spend the summer with him. I also would go back during the university's winter break and see him then. Of course, as he got older he was less interested in spending time with me. When he became a teenager he was more interested in hanging out with his friends and going on dates with girls. I haven't been to Sweden in three summers. He's visited here for a week here and there but it's not the same. I missed his childhood. We don't really know each other as a father and son should."

Jansson adjusted in his seat and finally looked at Chelsea, removing his gaze from the unknown object he had fixated on for the past few minutes. His face was inscrutable but his eyes shone with a sort of resigned sadness.

Chelsea had never seen Jansson so raw and undone. Normally he was the model of composure. She didn't want to impose on his pain, but she couldn't stop herself from asking him about one very important point.

"Then why did you leave?"

The question hung in the air between them like the misty vapor of a ghost caught between two worlds.

Jansson's brow furrowed more deeply.

"It all made sense to me then. I thought the damage was done...I didn't want him growing up with parents who hated each other and insulted one another in front of him, and I knew that's how it would be with me and Margit. I know how toxic that is for a child. I was so angry with her for what she did, I knew it would be hard to co-parent with her, and since she can't keep a civil tongue in her head about me, I knew we were in for an ugly battle. Also, I had already resigned my job at the university and accepted the position here. All those reasons seemed to be justified back then, but seem like very poor excuses now. The fact is I left my son."

Chelsea swallowed.

"You couldn't go back after a few years?" she asked. She didn't know why she was asking this. It wasn't her business, but she felt like she needed to know his reasoning, to understand his choice.

"Certainly I *could* have," Jansson said, his voice now sounding hollow. "But I didn't. There was always a reason, always an excuse not to leave Scranton...tenure, my students, I had bought a house here and obtained permanent residency in this country. I could have gone back and tried to make everything right but I never did. I couldn't. What must you think of me now?"

He pushed back his hair looking truly miserable, his pale blue eyes boring into her, for the first time piercing, filled with ache and self-loathing.

After a moment of silence he said "You didn't think I could be so terrible, did you?"

Chelsea felt an aching all her own.

"I think we all have it in us to be terrible," she said softly, a painful lump rising in her throat.

ᗡᖇ

When Chelsea went to bed that night, she lay awake long after she meant to be asleep, her thoughts swirling around her head. Thoughts of her own family...what was left of it, anyway. After her mother's death, it was just her and her father.

Unfortunately Marybeth had died at the same time Chelsea had needed to stretch her legs and see what life was like outside her household, or at least that's what she had convinced herself at the time. When she and Gene should have been leaning on one another, supporting each other in their mutual loss, Chelsea had wanted only to be on her own. She detached herself from a father with whom she had always been close, and a home where she had always been loved and in which she had never felt unwelcome. That is, of course, until she met Greg.

Jansson sat before her earlier that evening and spoke about his regrets, his choice to leave his son, his admission of how much he had failed as a father, and she could see how it hurt him, how guilty he felt for his choices. If Jansson was terrible, then Chelsea was just as guilty and just as terrible, if not more so. She, too, made the choice to leave, and like Jansson, now couldn't explain why, although she knew she had felt justified in her choice at the time.

She imagined how different her world might have been if her brother had lived. How old would he be now? She couldn't think. Eleven or twelve, she supposed. He would still be living at home with her dad. Her father wouldn't be in that house all alone. Chelsea would have someone to talk to about Marybeth, someone who understood the loss of a mother the way Chelsea did. Maybe her life would have turned out differently if her parents had another child to focus their attention on besides Chelsea. Or perhaps having a brother would have forced her to learn how to share and think of someone besides herself. She might be a different person today if baby Alexander had lived.

She thought about her father, so much like Jansson; living alone, separated from his only child who, with adulthood, had found other interests and ways to spend his time. She wondered if the sad emptiness she saw in Jansson's pale blue eyes resonated in her own father's face.

21

★ ★ ★

Gene heard a knock at the front door. He wasn't expecting anyone, but he figured it must be someone he knew because they did not use the doorbell. Or perhaps maybe they tried the bell and it had finally kicked the bucket, making knocking was the only option.

Gene made his way slowly to the door. He was remarkably calm when he opened it and saw Patrick Frye standing before him once again.

"Before you say anything, I just want to say I'm not here to bother you, I'd just like to apologize to you before I leave town. I did you wrong Mr. Shepherd, and I want you to know I'm sorry and can admit it."

This was of course, the last thing Gene expected to hear out of Patrick, short of him announcing he was joining a nude satanic cult in Zanzibar. But he found himself to be somewhat impressed that Patrick seemed to want to make amends. Gene knew Patrick Frye had been out of line. But he was back to his usual self, much calmer, and he felt it would be unfair to dismiss Patrick, who appeared sincerely apologetic, without hearing him out. He also knew he thoroughly deserved this apology and was determined to hear it out. He would let Patrick speak, but Patrick would also have to learn to listen.

Standing upright and looking Gene directly in the eye, Patrick began to speak.

"I was wrong to discuss your very personal business with your neighbor. She should not have divulged that sort of information about you and your family, and I should never have spoken about it to you as a means to help you find Jesus. You're right; when it comes down to it, I don't know you from Adam, and had no right to speak about people and situations I know nothing about."

There was silence as Gene let Patrick's mea culpa sink in. He didn't know what had opened Patrick's eyes, since most reasonable people would have recognized that Patrick's actions were wrong in the first place. Whether it was because he had been the victim of the eruption of Gene's temper, or if he had come to this conclusion in another way, Gene was glad Patrick had at last realized his approach was flawed. Gene found himself able to accept Patrick's apology. But now it was his turn to talk.

"I appreciate you saying all that. Your apology is accepted. But we have to straighten a few things out. You told me once that you enjoy having religious discussions and hearing other people's point of view," Gene said steadily.

"Yes sir, I did," replied Patrick. He was treading very carefully, and making a clear effort to be extra respectful.

"But that's not really true, Patrick. You think you're being open-minded, but all you do is wait in polite silence until the other person is done talking. You're really only waiting for him to finish speaking his piece so you can get to yours. You take none of it in. You may hear what somebody is saying, but you're not *listening*. Then you just dig your heels in and insist that your beliefs are absolute truth simply because that's what you were brought up to believe."

"I am very secure in my faith. I know in my heart that these things are true. But I suppose you're right, I don't hear other people's views with a truly open mind. I suppose all I do is listen to them make an argument because I'm confident I can counter it. It's just that I believe this so strongly, and I know all the good it does and how it enriches my life and the lives of others. I contest their arguments because I want others to have the happiness that comes with being sound in one's beliefs."

"Well I never asked for that happiness. I never invited you into my life, yet you kept coming back. It was completely out of line for you to come back here and discuss my family, especially after I'd asked you to leave me alone." Gene could not believe he had to scold the young man, especially after he had blown up at Patrick so intensely the last time he was there. He spoke gently, but sternly.

Patrick, to his credit, appeared to be sincerely contrite.

"I realize that now. And I apologize for interfering in your private affairs. It's just that I hope one day to be a pastor, and pastors are supposed to be able to help people with their family problems." For the first time since Gene had met Patrick, the young man looked embarrassed. His eyes were cast downward, and his body looked strangely bent, almost stooped in resignation.

"Pastors are only responsible for helping members of their congregations. And that's only if those members *want* help." Gene wasn't sure whether Patrick would ever truly understand how much he was in the wrong. But Gene was not going to let Patrick walk away without listening to what he had to say, whether Patrick wanted to hear it or not. Gene had done his fair share of listening.

"Yes sir, I suppose you're right. I know I told you I was making rounds and visiting folks around here. I made it seem like I was going door-to-door. This was misleading. I dropped by several houses but no one really talked to me other than Mrs. List that one time. The truth is, yours is the only house I visited more than once."

Gene already suspected this. By not sending Patrick on his way after his first visit, he had given him hope that Gene would be his special project, and he was certain no other person would open the door for him more than once as he had.

"I see," was all Gene said. "You mind telling me why I became your own personal cause?"

"You seemed to be alone Mr. Shepherd. I thought maybe, even if you didn't accept Jesus into your life, you might accept another human being." With this, Patrick finally looked up at Gene, right into his face. His look was questioning, almost sad and his cheeks were slightly red.

There was silence between them. Gene did not know how to react to such a statement.

Patrick was right. He *was* alone.

No Marybeth.

No Chelsea.

His parents were both dead and his brother gone, probably for good. He had been utterly unable to surround himself with friends or even family for almost a year. He spent most of his days at work in the garage repairing tractors and hardly any time interacting with the clientele. He really had shut himself off from the rest of the world.

Patrick was absolutely not the person Gene would have chosen to provide him with the company or even the basic human interaction that a person needs. But hadn't Gene been more actively involved with friends since meeting Patrick? Hadn't he been more acutely aware of his solitary lifestyle? And why *had* he continued to interact with Patrick?

He had opened the door for the young man more than once, allowed Patrick to engage him in conversation, however frustrating and infuriating it had been to hear his religious preaching. He had threatened more than once to press charges for trespassing, yet he never did. Gene, at more than six feet tall and over two-hundred pounds, had developed strength that came from having done physical labor for more than half of his life. If he had wanted to physically remove Patrick from his property, he could have easily done so at any time. Yet he hadn't.

Maybe he had needed someone to talk to besides Maudie, someone who could talk back. Maybe he needed a conversation that wasn't about tractor parts or ordering supplies or home improvement products. Even if that meant verbal sparring with a twenty-one-year-old self-professed Jesus freak. Gene realized that for all Patrick's faults, his stubborn resolve to save everyone's soul, his cavalier attitude that he knew best about God and the universe and his annoying self-importance, it was better than silence. It was better than talking to no one. It made Gene feel something besides loss and loneliness, even if it was irritation and resentment towards the person invading his solitude. And in his own twisted, misguided way, deep down, Patrick Frye had meant well.

To Patrick's great surprise Gene chuckled.

"You told me you were making rounds and I was the only one who you bothered more than once? Patrick you lied. You lied in an attempt to have me accept Jesus? What would He think of you lying in His name?"

"I apologize for that Mr. Shepherd. My WWJD manual is a little unclear on the topic of deception in the name of saving souls," Patrick said seriously.

WWJD manual? Gene thought. *Why did that sound familiar? Unless…*

"Patrick…did you just make a What Would Jesus Do joke?"

Finally Patrick grinned and said, "Yes sir, I did. Even Christians can have a sense of humor. But I'm not perfect, and I know how devout Christians can seem to secular people. I can't be one-hundred percent good, one-hundred percent of the time, only Jesus can do that. The best I can do is try."

Gene stared unblinkingly, doubting whether anything Patrick Frye could do or say would shock him after that.

Patrick sat in the chair next to Gene. He sat up straight, not looking too comfortable but determined to speak his mind.

"I'm not just a crusader, Mr. Shepherd. I feel like everyone is put on this planet for a reason. And I believe my purpose is to spread the word to others that there *is* a purpose. I took this domestic missionary assignment because I knew I couldn't live in a world that was meaningless, and I wanted to be able to show more people who are jaded by apathy and cold, hard science that it's not all for nothing. I can't stand the idea that people think all this," he waved his hand around him distractedly, "is an accident of biology. That would mean that nothing we feel or think or even experience really matters. I don't want to live like that. Believing there's no greater purpose, that our lives can all be explained away with chemicals and empirical science. I can't live like that."

Gene sat down on the porch chair. Except for the domestic missionary bit and the part about needing to spread the word, Gene knew exactly what Patrick meant. It was the same feeling he'd had as a child looking up at the stars in that terrifying moment when he doubted the existence of God.

"I never said there wasn't a greater meaning to life. You never actually asked me what I believe. I agree with you, Patrick, about there being a bigger purpose. I just don't show it in the same way you do. People can show their appreciation for life's meaning and purpose in more than one way, and just because some of them shut out Christianity and organized religion, doesn't mean they are shutting out God."

Patrick nodded slowly. "It seems I've got a lot to think about," he said, sincerely. "I'm going back to Utah to meet with other missionaries to discuss our experiences. Then I might do some missionary work abroad. Either way, I have a feeling I'm going to have to change my approach to helping others see what I see."

"Good for you, Patrick," Gene said. And he genuinely meant it. "I would just ask you to respect when a person has different beliefs than you. If they are still not open to what you have to say after you've given it the old college try, accept that, and move on."

"I'll keep that in mind," Patrick said.

"You know, there are other forums where you can discuss spiritual and philosophical issues besides pestering people in their homes. Places where people enjoy the debate and learn and grow." Gene said. He still hoped to nudge Patrick towards an approach to his mission that did not boarder on harassment.

"I will have to look into something like that," Patrick said, "Anyhow," he continued, getting to his feet, "I'm leaving in the next few days, and I just wanted to apologize for infringing on your personal business. I didn't want to leave without setting things right. I thought it would be the Christian thing to do...apologize, that is."

"Thank you," Gene said, and then added "I think you and I are finally beginning to understand each other."

Before turning to leave Patrick offered his hand to Gene, and Gene shook it. Without another word Patrick swiftly walked down the front steps and across the driveway towards the street. Gene stood there watching until the young man was out of sight.

22

★ ★ ★

The holidays were right around the corner. Gene was now facing his first Thanksgiving and Christmas without Marybeth, and presumably, since he hadn't heard otherwise, without Chelsea. He had been silently dreading the impending holiday season for quite some time. Try as he might to avoid thinking about it, the fact was that Thanksgiving loomed before him, only a few days away.

Tom and Sharon invited him to their house for Thanksgiving dinner, and he supposed that he would end up there. He knew they meant well and that they loved him as family. He loved them as well and appreciated all their support, but somehow didn't necessarily feel up to being surrounded by Marybeth's relatives; not just yet, anyway. He had seen her parents only once since her funeral because they lived in Florida, and her siblings only a handful of times more than that even though Tom and Sharon lived just outside Philly and Mitch and his family lived in New Jersey. He felt it would be easier to get together with them on a regular weekend rather than a holiday, when there wasn't so much pressure and Marybeth's absence wasn't so raw.

Plus, it would feel strange to be there without Chelsea, whose Thanksgiving plans were a mystery to him. As far as he knew from the few times he'd spoken with her since the day Greg came to the shop looking for her, she was still "staying with a friend and trying to figure things out"...whatever "things" were.

Luckily Gene was spared having to make a decision about Thanksgiving at Tom and Sharon's house in the end. As it turned out, Ron Sciaruto's soon-to-be ex-wife was getting their boys for Thanksgiving (Ron would spend a Thanksgiving-like day with the kids on Black Friday) so, not wanting to spend the day alone, Ron called Gene up and invited him to spend the afternoon and evening drinking with him at Sully's. Gene happily accepted, and the two spent hours eating buffalo-wings, drinking lagers, and watching various football games on the different screens all around the bar.

Like father, like daughter; Chelsea also spent her Thanksgiving Day in a less-than-traditional fashion. Jansson, being Swedish, did not usually celebrate Thanksgiving, although as he told Chelsea, he had experienced several Thanksgiving dinners over the years when he had been invited to his friends' homes. He offered to go out and buy the traditional Thanksgiving foods with all the trimmings so he and Chelsea could attempt to cook the meal.

"What do you think, we could make a day of it...cooking and then eating?"

Chelsea thought the offer was very sweet, but she still declined it. She was not in a place emotionally where she could have a Thanksgiving dinner and deal with all the memories she had of past Thanksgivings with her parents and Danielle's family. She knew a big traditional meal would serve as a glaring reminder that this was her first Thanksgiving since her mom died, and she was already battling against the guilt she felt for not planning to spend the day with her father. As much as she knew the choice would hurt her dad, she still didn't feel she could face him and deal with all their complicated issues yet, especially not on a family holiday. *Just another item to add to the Reasons Why I'm a Crappy Daughter List*, she thought.

She also didn't want to think about the implications of the holiday; giving thanks when her head was in such a funny place and her still-secret pregnancy weighed heavily on her mind. She didn't think going home and saying "Happy first Thanksgiving without Mom, Dad! Oh, by the way, I'm pregnant, and Greg's probably the father!"

Instead, she and Jansson splurged and ordered an obscene amount of Mexican food from a small authentic place called Taberna de Dos Hermanos that had the most outstanding enchiladas. They had a lovely non-Thanksgiving day eating the food (which would last as leftovers for days) and watching foreign films that were old favorites of Jansson's that he was excited to show Chelsea.

The next morning, Chelsea braced herself for Black Friday. Although she would never go out shopping on a day of such commercial hysteria, the day after Thanksgiving always marked the unofficial countdown to Christmas. If Chelsea thought Thanksgiving would be difficult to get through in her current predicament, she dreaded to think of how she was going to navigate through a month of yuletide cheer.

❦

Despite being certain she was not ready to talk about the baby to her father or Jansson, Chelsea found that she couldn't keep the knowledge completely to herself. She really needed to talk to about her situation with someone. So far, the only other person who knew about her pregnancy was Brooke, and she knew Brooke wouldn't judge her or talk about her personal business to anyone else. Brooke also had a young child of her own, so calling her made a lot of sense.

But when Chelsea reached for her phone, she found her fingers instinctively dialing a different number. She waited while it rang.

"Hey, stranger," came Danielle's voice, audibly glad to be hearing from her cousin.

"Hi, Danielle. I'm so sorry; it really has been a long time since we talked."

"No kidding," Danielle returned. She didn't sound judgmental or angry, just matter-of-fact. "How have you been?"

"Well," Chelsea half-laughed, "A lot's been going on..."

"Tell me."

Chelsea knew how Danielle felt about Greg, so she was pretty sure that Danielle would be glad to hear they were not longer together. Although Danielle did have her opinions, she was an exceptionally good confidant.

"I broke up with Greg."

There was a pause.

"Go on..." Danielle said. She was not about to jump for joy and dive right into Greg-bashing if there was any chance this was one of those break-up, then make-up situations. Danielle liked to have all the information first.

Chelsea took a deep breath and started her story.

"Well last time I talked to you I think I mentioned he was partying a lot and we weren't really spending time together, you know, as like, a couple. Things had been steadily going downhill for months, really. He was drinking and snorting coke pretty much on the regular, and we were fighting all the time." She swallowed as her words came rushing out from her, and she was relieved to be able to really talk about it with someone.

"I kept trying to make it work, and excuse it away, and hoping it would change, but it didn't, he just got worse. And mean. He got really nasty. It wasn't the same anymore. *He* wasn't the same. Then one night during a huge fight he hit me..."

" —I will hire a hit man."

"No, no. There's no need for that. I walked out right then and there and haven't looked back since. We're done. I am never going back to that."

"Are you sure?" Danielle asked cautiously. "Sometimes people reconcile…"

"Not this time. That's damage you just can't fix. And he's not good for me. He's not good for my life. Whatever I've been doing lately, it hasn't been working, so I'm really looking to turn over a new leaf."

There was another pause.

"Is this for real, Chels?"

"Definitely. That guy I fell in love with…he's gone. Greg's a totally different person now. A person I don't want in my life."

Danielle let out a hugely audible sigh of relief.

"THANK. GOD. Do you know how long we've all been waiting for you to come to your senses? This is the best news I've heard in ages. I want to send you balloons. I want to dance in the streets shouting *SO LONG, SUCKER!*"

Chelsea laughed. She did know how long her family had been waiting for this. She was happy she had made a major step towards a different life, and it was clear Danielle was, too.

"So what's your plan now, are you back with your dad? We missed you at Thanksgiving."

Chelsea squirmed. Another reminder of the long list of things she already felt guilty about.

"Not yet. I'm staying with a friend for now, but I am definitely headed back home really soon."

"Chelsea…"

"I promise, I've just got to sort some stuff out then I'm headed back home for sure. That's where I belong right now and I know it."

"About time, too," Danielle scolded gently. She thought about stopping there since Chelsea was already planning to go home, but decided against it. She had more to say, and her cousin wasn't going to get out of this scot-free.

"Your father *really* misses you, Chels," she said seriously. "He's all alone in that house. I went to see him earlier in the semester. He's doing the best he can and putting up a good front, but he's lonely and needs you. He needs family. He's still grieving for your mom…"

"I know," Chelsea said, shame rising painfully in her chest as her face flushed. She wanted to say *I am, too* but found that she had suppressed her own grief for so long that she now realized she probably had a long way to go herself where grieving was concerned. She supposed this was another hurdle she would have to deal with upon moving back in with her dad. She worried that once she opened that door and confronted all the feelings she had been pushing away for so long, she might fall apart completely, and she needed to do that at home, with her father. She knew she was looking at a tough road ahead, but it was one she was willing, and more importantly, wanting to take.

"I swear. I'll be back on Hopikon Road by the end of next weekend."

"Good," said Danielle with a note of finality in her voice.

Chelsea thought about asking Danielle how everything was with her and how school was going before sharing more news with her, but she couldn't hold the words in much longer.

"So...I have to tell you something else."

"Okay..." said Danielle, immediately growing concerned at the sudden seriousness in Chelsea's tone.

"But it has to stay between you and me for now. You can't tell your parents or my dad. Please."

"You know I won't tell."

Chelsea thought it would be easier saying the words, but realized even though she was desperate to tell someone, she had never said it out loud before.

"I'm pregnant," she said. There it was. Out in the open. It was real, and now Danielle knew it, too.

"You're *what?*"

"I found out a couple weeks ago. You're the only one who knows other than my friend who bought me the pregnancy test."

There was another long pause from Danielle. Her brain felt addled. There were so many questions to ask, she didn't know where to begin.

"Well, what are you going to do?"

Chelsea paused for a moment, then said with such certainty and clarity that she took even herself by surprise, "I'm keeping it."

"Okay then," said Danielle, and Chelsea knew she had her cousin's complete support.

Chelsea felt a bit dazed. She hadn't been aware until this conversation that despite all the confusion and fear she'd felt since she first saw the little pink plus sign, whether or not she would keep her baby had never been a question. From the moment the test had turned up positive, she had known deep down in her gut this was her baby. She was going to be a mother and the panic she had been feeling was about how to handle this new curve ball life had thrown at her, not about the baby itself. Looking back at the past few weeks she realized her anxiety and indecision had never been about what she was going to do about the pregnancy. It was always about what she was going to do about her life now that she would soon have a child.

"And what about Greg?" came Danielle's voice, jerking Chelsea's thoughts back to the present. "You can't raise a kid with someone who hits you. And even if he hadn't, Greg's not fit to be a father."

"Trust me, I know. I'm not planning on telling him about it. At least for now, anyway."

She decided to leave Jansson and that whole mess out of the conversation completely. She was not prepared to cross that bridge, and she didn't want Danielle's brain to collapse from her life-drama overload.

"Oh my God," Danielle sighed. "I thought you guys were, you know, being safe. Aren't you on birth control?"

Chelsea wasn't surprised that this was the direction Danielle was going after hearing her news. Even when they were growing up, Danielle had always been the motherly one and wasn't shy about calling Chelsea out. This question didn't bother Chelsea. She had always been responsible in the contraception department and knew that under normal circumstances, she would never have forgotten to use protection.

"I was, but when I left Greg, I forgot to take my prescription with me and we'd been sleeping together regularly. It must have just been the really wrong time in my cycle to stop taking them."

"Okay, fair enough. These things happen. Have you been to the doctor yet?"

"No. Not yet. I've been really frazzled lately, and I—"

"Chelsea you need to make an appointment with an OBGYN as soon as possible."

In all honesty, Chelsea hadn't even thought about seeing her doctor. Her cheeks started to flush again with embarrassment and guilt. *Of course* she needed to make an appointment. She needed to look into pre-natal care and vitamins and making sure her health checked out okay. And the baby. She needed an ultrasound. She had to see if the baby was alright.

"You're right. I'll call tomorrow and see if I can get an appointment for next week. And then I've got to tell Dad."

"Good. Sounds like you're going to have one hell of a week."

"Yeah. God, I'm probably not even twelve weeks pregnant and already I'm screwing up as a mom."

Danielle's voice softened.

"No," she said into the phone, "You're just nineteen and freaked out."

"Freaked out is an understatement."

"Sorry, Cuz," Danielle said playfully. "Looks like you've become just another teenage pregnancy statistic."

"Thanks a lot." Chelsea said.

"Seriously, though. Go home. Talk to your dad. I'm sure he can help support you with this. He wouldn't want you dealing with it alone."

"I will. I promise."

"Keep me updated, okay?" Danielle said.

"I will. I'm done keeping my family at arm's length. And I kind of have no choice but to deal with everything and get my shit together, so I'm going to."

"I'm very glad to hear it."

"Thanks, Danielle. Love you."

"Anytime, babes. Love you, too."

The weather was now very cold. It had snowed a few times, and although none of the snow accumulated on the ground, everything outside seemed to be frozen. Chelsea woke up on that Saturday morning completely rested, and for the first time since she could remember, her mind was crystal clear.

The heating in Jansson's house wasn't always very dependable, and that morning it was particularly cold. She threw on a sweatshirt and wrapped a blanket around herself before heading out of her room into the kitchen. Jansson was already there, sitting at the table drinking coffee and reading the newspaper.

Chelsea slid into the chair across the table from Jansson.

"Good morning," she said.

"Good morning," he replied, smiling as he turned the page of his paper. "I was thinking of getting a fire going in the fire place in a few minutes, what do you think?"

"Sounds good to me," Chelsea said, tightening the blanket around her.

"Would you like some breakfast?"

"Oh I'll just pour myself some cereal, thanks," she replied.

Jansson resumed reading the paper.

Chelsea bit her lower lip. She wasn't sure how to begin what she wanted to say.

"I've been doing some thinking," Chelsea said finally.

Jansson looked up with a small jerk. He hoped Chelsea hadn't noticed. From the tone in her voice he knew before she said anything else what she was thinking.

"I think I need to go home...to my dad."

"I see," Jansson said softly.

"You have been so good to me. You took me in. You gave me a place to stay. You've been a wonderful friend. I would stay here indefinitely if I could. But while I'm here, I'm avoiding figuring my life out. I need to go back to work, or at least find out if I want to go to school."

"I think you would like school, Chelsea. I think it would be a great experience for you and you would do very well there." Jansson's eyes looked sad, but he knew she was right, that she couldn't stay with him forever.

"I also have to make things right with my dad. I have some serious atoning to do. I don't know how I'm going to even begin to make up with him, but I need to try. I realized I'm not just mixed up about my future; I'm mixed up about everything. And I think the best way for me to work out what I want is for me to figure out who I am, without Greg, back in the house where I grew up, with help from my family."

Chelsea felt the need to explain herself, to defend her decision. She knew Jansson would be supportive and understanding, he always was. But she couldn't help feeling that by leaving Jansson's house, she was hurting him somehow. She would return home to her lonely father to try and pick up the pieces of their lives, but would be leaving behind another lonely man whom she had given and received companionship and for whom cared for a great deal.

"You don't have to explain, my dear, I support your decision. You're young. You should find your calling and live your life." Jansson looked directly into her eyes.

Chelsea looked back into his kind face, at his pale eyes gazing at her and she suppressed a shiver that had nothing to do with how cold she felt. She could not tell him about the baby. She needed to see a doctor, find out how far along she really was in order to determine who it belonged to before she could explain her pregnancy. She had to work out her exact feelings for Jansson, for there were feelings, but she could not define them. She thought perhaps with distance she could figure out what she really felt.

Jansson surveyed Chelsea. He knew if she was ready to leave, then it was truly time for her to go home but his heart felt heavy none the less. He would be alone once again. They would never discuss that night in his bed. He would have to let her go.

"I still want to see you," she said suddenly.

"I would like that very much," Jansson said. "Even if you don't live here, we can still be friends. I will always be your friend."

"And I'll always be yours," she said back, her eyes shining with earnestness.

Jansson stood up put his hand on Chelsea's shoulder and lightly kissed her forehead.

"I'm going to get that fire started. When do you think you will you call your father and tell him you're coming home?"

"Tomorrow," Chelsea said. "I'll move back home in the next few days. I'm in no rush. That is, if he'll take me back in."

"He will," Jansson said, "Don't worry, he will."

23

✳ ✳ ✳

I t was snowing. A fresh white blanket had accumulated about two inches on the ground already and the weather channel report that Foothills could get over a foot that night.

Gene wasn't bothered by this news, as he didn't have anywhere to go that evening. He would be fine with his wood-burning stove, some hot beef stew, and a good book. It was Friday night, so he could wake up the next morning and shovel the driveway whenever he felt like it without having to worry about getting to work on time. Tonight he could just sit back, relax, and appreciate the beauty of winter.

He went out to the garage to get some logs from his stack of firewood and had to practically drag Maudie down the front steps. She whined and gave him a pathetic look. For some reason unknown to Gene, Maudie had huge issues with snow. Getting her outside to take care of her business in the winter months was always a challenge and tonight was no exception. She parked herself on the bottom step and stared doubtfully at the white powder covering the lawn. While other neighborhood dogs bounced around in snow banks with joyous abandon, Maudie regarded the fluffy, cold precipitation as though it were both alien and hazardous. Gene happened to think this was simultaneously funny and ridiculous as Maudie had no such issues with rain, any kind of water, or even mud.

He brought the firewood inside and returned to the porch where Maudie still looked as though she were worried that if she ventured onto the lawn, she might never return from its snowy doom. Gene finally took pity on her and cleared the snow off of a square yard of grass with a shovel. *Well, what the heck?* he thought. *She's the perfect dog in every other aspect and she's getting old. Why not indulge her for this one quirk.* Maudie was only somewhat mollified, but she used the clear patch to do her business and then scrambled back up the steps and onto the porch.

It was almost midnight and Gene was well-immersed in his book when the phone rang and shook him from his concentration.

Gene picked up the phone.

"Gene. Ron Sciaruto."

"Hey, Ron. What's going on?" It was pretty late for any calls. He sensed a serious note in his friend's voice and braced himself.

"Have you talked to Chelsea recently?" Ron asked.

Gene felt fear rise swiftly in his chest. When a cop called you at home this late and asked about your daughter, even a cop who was a friend, it was never to tell you good news.

"Yes, this afternoon briefly during my lunch break. Why?"

"Because I need to be in touch with her and the apartment she has with Greg doesn't have a land line. Could you give me her cell number?"

"Chelsea hasn't been living there for several weeks. She's staying with a friend. She and Greg aren't together anymore." Gene was very pleased to announce this.

"I see. Well I think she should know Greg's been in a serious car accident. They took him to the St. Giles' a few minutes ago."

"Oh man," Gene said. He didn't like Greg one bit, but he would never wish serious harm on anyone. "How bad?"

"Bad," Ron replied. "So even if he and Chelsea are broken up, she might want to know about it."

"Okay..."

"There's something else, Gene."

Gene felt a jolt in his chest. What else could it be if Chelsea wasn't involved? Gene knew she was safely staying in tonight, she had told him earlier that day she'd be watching movies all night with her friend.

"Remember you told me about that Christian kid who kept bugging you?"

"Yeah. Patrick Frye..." Gene said slowly.

"When Greg's car spun, he hit a pedestrian walking by the side of the road before he collided with a tree. The pedestrian; it's that kid, Gene. It's Patrick. He was struck as Greg skidded off of the road. This is police business; I'm not supposed to be giving out names like this, but Frye isn't from around here and we haven't been able to get in touch with his family back in Utah. Besides, I thought you should know. You mentioned him. They took him to the hospital, too."

Gene was silent. He just listened to the static of the phone.

"It doesn't look good, Gene," Ron said.

"Okay. Thanks for calling, Ron. Don't worry about getting in touch with Chelsea. I'll call her right now. It's better if she hears it from me."

He hung up the phone.

Maudie followed him as he stepped out onto the porch. It was still snowing heavily and the temperature was plummeting by the hour. His yard was now covered with what appeared to be six or seven inches. His breath caught in his chest as the frigid air hit his lungs. Big, fat snowflakes falling at impressive speeds obscured his vision as he looked up into the sky. He couldn't see any stars.

Chelsea continued to hold her cell phone in her hand long after she hung up with her dad. She felt as though her heart had stopped with a jolt of electricity when Gene said "car accident" and "hospital." Now it was pumping again, this time at full force, harder and faster than she thought a human heart could beat. It was as though her heart were a boxing glove hammering against her chest, trying to break free from her ribcage. In the two minutes that she had spoken to her dad, her stomach had twisted into a gigantic knot and her blood had turned to lead in her veins.

Jansson was still in the kitchen making popcorn and hot cocoa when the call came. They were spending one of their last few nights together watching back-to-back Alfred Hitchcock films while the snow piled up outside.

When he returned minutes later with a tray, he found Chelsea sitting as still as a statue, staring straight ahead. Her eyes unfocused and her hand out in front of her holding her cell phone as though it was a time-bomb.

"What's wrong? What happened? You look like you just saw a ghost," Jansson said. He put down the tray then moved toward her with growing concern and gently put a hand on her shoulder.

"My dad just called," Chelsea said, appearing to awaken from her shocked trance. "Greg was an accident. He crashed the car into a tree."

Jansson sat down next to her on the couch, scrutinizing her face.

"Is he alright?" he asked.

"No," Chelsea said, her voice abrupt and almost cold. She swallowed, took a steadying breath and then continued more calmly, "They took him right to the ER. My dad says he's in bad shape. Dad's good friends with a Foothills cop who called to let him know, and Officer Sciaruto says...he says..." her throat seemed to close up painfully before she could get anything else out.

"Do you want me to drive you to the hospital?" Jansson offered quietly.

Without thinking Chelsea nodded furtively.

"I've got to go put on some jeans and some warm clothes first," she said. She was already in her pajamas.

"Of course," said Jansson, standing up.

Chelsea sat immobile for a moment before springing into action. She went to the office and ransacked her massive duffle for her boots and some gloves. She couldn't find any gloves so she grabbed a scarf. The only boots she had taken from the apartment were bright pink rain boots with daisies on them—totally inappropriate for both the weather and the grim situation. *Oh well*, she thought, throwing on an extra pair of socks for warmth, *better than nothing*. When she walked into the foyer, Jansson was already wearing a thick puffy jacket and a winter hat.

She stopped in her tracks.

"I don't love him anymore," she declared.

"You don't have to explain," Jansson said, looking slightly taken aback. He felt his heart skip a beat, wondering where she was going with this.

"But should I be going there even after everything? After how we broke up? Is it my place to sit in the waiting room with his family to hear if he's going to..." she paused. She couldn't say *die*. She swallowed and instead said "Be okay?"

Jansson stood silently for a moment.

"I think you know the answer to that," he said. "You might not love him now. But you loved him once. And going to see if he's going to be alright doesn't mean you want to get back together with him. It just means you care."

It was true. Chelsea knew she had to go to the hospital. She had dated Greg for two years, loved him, lived with him, and he was very likely the father of her baby. However he had changed, however badly he had treated her, she knew she had to be there to see what happened to him.

"You're right. Let's go."

She layered her peacoat over a warm sweater and wrapped her hands in her scarf.

"Don't be silly," Jansson said, walking towards his hall closet and pulling out a pair of his own gloves. He handed them to Chelsea, who gratefully pulled them on, although they were much too big. She wrapped the scarf around her neck instead.

Jansson held the door open for her. The snow was still falling in great clumps and covered several inches of Jansson's porch. It was intensely quiet. The world outside looked picturesque and tranquil like a winter wonderland Christmas card. Before she could step out into the night, she turned to Jansson, still holding the door ajar.

"There's something else," she said.

"What do you mean, Chelsea?"

"When Greg crashed the car, he hit someone."

"Another car? Was someone else involved in the crash?"

"Not another car," Chelsea said darkly. "Before he crashed into the tree he hit a man walking by the side of the road."

Without waiting for a reaction, she marched out the door and began to wade through the thick snow towards Jansson's garage.

Jansson remained where he stood in stunned silence for beat, and then briskly followed Chelsea out into the winter's night.

Chelsea was glad Jansson drove a Ford Explorer. The snow continued to rain down around them, and Jansson had to put his wipers on full blast. The plows had been out already, but the falling flakes seemed to be replacing the cleared snow in no time at all. It was also the worst kind of snow drive on, the light, powdery, crystal fluff that refuses to be packed into a snowball or a snowman, and is slick under car tires.

She felt much more secure making the drive, which through Foothills was a quite curvy and hill-filled journey, in Jansson's midnight blue four-wheel-drive beast of an SUV than she would have in the Subaru sedan that she and Greg used to share. Because it was late at night and the weather was so terrible, there were few cars on the road. The occasional cars that passed them moved slowly and swerved often as they tried to maneuver the ups and downs of the roadway. The hospital was just under thirty minutes away, but given the de-creased visibility and slickness of the pavement, Jansson drove below the speed limit and gave the cars in front and behind them a very wide berth. They passed at least two cars that had lost their bat-tle against the weather. One car was stopped diag-onally in the middle of the opposite lane with its hazard lights flashing, and another seemed to be stuck in an embankment by one of the side streets.

Although she was eager to get to the hospital, Chelsea was glad they were in no rush. She wasn't sure how she would be able to handle the situation once they arrived. Greg's family would be there which would mean she could be in for some awk-ward explaining about the current state of her rela-tionship with Greg. She also worried about her ability to cope with intense situations. Who knew what news they might get from the doctors?

"What would you like me to do when we get there?" Jansson asked, jerking Chelsea's thoughts back to the present. He wanted to be there to support her, but knew she might need some space. This was her ex-boyfriend, one who had abused her. The situation was delicate.

She considered this for a moment.

"Well...I know I don't want you to drop me off. I'd want you to be there in case I needed you. But his parents will be there. I should probably deal with them alone. I don't know. This might sound like a lot to ask, but...do you think you could stick around but maybe not in the ER? Just don't leave me there." She turned to look at him.

"It's not a problem," he said. "I can buy something to read in the gift shop and stay in the main lobby. I think there's a Starbucks in there as well. You can call me if you need me and I'll join you in Emergency. Sound good?"

Chelsea smiled weakly. Jansson always seemed to know exactly what to do in these situations and somehow always managed to give her exactly what she needed without her having to ask. He was so good to her she felt she didn't quite deserve it.

"Yes, that sounds good. Thank you, Alexander."

24

When they finally pulled up to the emergency entrance of St. Giles' Memorial Hospital, Jansson dropped Chelsea off at the curb.

"Remember, just call when you need me," he said.

"I will."

She hopped down from his enormous car and trudged through the snow towards the automatic sliding doors. Her toes immediately felt the biting cold through her plastic boots. As she neared the entrance, she saw a thin woman with graying brown hair smoking a cigarette next to a bench to the side of the sliding doors. She wasn't wearing a winter coat, only a gray fleece and judging by the number of butts at her feet she'd been through several cigarettes, despite the sign directly behind her reading *NO SMOKING NEAR HOSPITAL ENTRANCE.* Chelsea recognized her at once. It was Therese Townsend, Greg's mother, and she paced and bounced up and down trying to keep warm while she chain-smoked.

Chelsea approached her.

"Chels!" Therese threw down the butt she had been smoking and engulfed Chelsea in a fierce hug. She smelled just as Chelsea remembered: of tobacco and mint, from the endless breath mints and pieces of gum Therese used to try and cover up her smoker's breathe. Chelsea returned the embrace.

"Have they told you anything?" she asked when they pulled apart.

"He's in surgery right now," Therese croaked, her voice like gravel from years of nicotine addiction. "They said something about internal hemorrhaging from the crash and head trauma." Her crinkled eyes began to tear.

"Oh my God..." Chelsea said. "Did they say how serious it was?"

"They said we have to see how the surgery goes." She gasped through a sob, then tried to compose herself. "They said his condition is critical. Now all we can do is pray. Honey, I'm so glad you're here. I tried calling you at your dad's house but there was no answer. When he showed up, he said you were on your way."

"My dad? He's here?" Chelsea couldn't believe her ears.

"Yeah, he got here fifteen minutes ago."

Chelsea hesitated for a moment, wanting to go inside to where her father was, but wasn't sure if she should leave Therese alone out in the snow.

"Go on in darlin', I just can't be in there with that hospital smell for too long. I'll be inside in a few."

Chelsea squeezed Therese's shoulder and then headed inside. The sliding door opened for her. She turned the corner and saw the waiting area, strangely empty for a Saturday night during a blizzard. Sitting in one of the chairs and looking over-large was Gene Shepherd. He looked up when he heard the squeaking, sticking sound of her boots as she walked in.

He stood up.

"Dad!" She rushed into his arms.

They held each other for a long time without speaking. Chelsea breathed in deep her dad's scent, the suede from his favorite jacket, the faint smell of a wood-burning stove, and her house, her home.

"What are you doing here?" she asked as they both took seats side by side.

"I thought you might need me," Gene said. It was only half true. Gene *knew* Chelsea would need him. However this night turned out, whatever happened to Greg, he knew his daughter needed him tonight.

"Thanks, Dad."

She leaned her head on his large shoulder.

"Good to see you, Bean."

"Have they told you anything?"

"I talked to Therese and Vick. He's in really serious condition, honey."

Chelsea took a deep breath.

"Should I be bracing myself?" she asked.

"There's always reason to hope. We should think positive. But yes, I would prepare for some bad news."

"Shit." Chelsea said. She could think of nothing eloquent to say that summed up her emotions more appropriately. She felt sick to her stomach and a burning in her chest.

"Do his parents know, I mean, did they say anything that indicated they know Greg and I broke up?" Chelsea wasn't sure getting left was the kind of news Greg would report back to Mom and Dad.

"Vick said they know you two aren't living together anymore but he was glad you were coming.

He said maybe you two could work things out. After...." Gene left the sentence hanging.

"Well. Good. I'm glad they know. But we're not getting back together. We are all wrong."

Gene just nodded.

"Do me a favor and wait until next week to tell me *I told you so*." Chelsea knew he was thinking it but would never actually say it.

"Of course," Gene said.

"So, what happened? How did this happen? Where was the accident? And is the other man alright?" Chelsea wanted all the details as soon as possible.

Gene took a deep breath. He had got some information from talking to Officer Sciaruto and to Greg's parents.

"I guess he was leaving a friend's house, they think to get more beer. There were a bunch of people there and they say he volunteered to go out. He had been drinking. I don't know if he was drunk, Vick didn't say anything about it and Ron can't give out details like that to me."

Chelsea knew Greg's dad wouldn't have mentioned to Gene if Greg was drunk anyway, given his own alcoholism. There was a fair amount of denial in the Townsend family about alcohol abuse. In fact, Chelsea would have bet all the money in her wallet that across the waiting room the Dr. Pepper Vick Townsend was now drinking was spiked.

"If he wasn't drunk I'm sure he was rolling anyway," Chelsea said in a low voice, not wanting Vick to hear. He sat several rows away facing the window, with his head in his hand and his eyes closed.

Gene raised an eyebrow.

"Rolling? Remind me which drug that is again, it's been a while since the sixties."

"It can refer to any number of drugs but with Greg, it's cocaine. He's got a serious coke habit. It's one of the reasons I left. So he went out to buy beer…what happened then?"

"He was driving on Hawthorne Road towards town through the snow when he lost control of the car. I guess he fishtailed and skidded off the road and that's where he collided with the tree. Car's totaled. They had to cut him out of it."

"Leave it to Greg to crash a car on the straightest, flattest road in Foothills," Chelsea observed bitterly. "Of course he wouldn't care that the roads were bad. Greg does what he wants, regardless of anyone or anything else."

Chelsea started tugging at the ends of her hair. She hadn't realized how angry she still was at Greg despite no longer being in love with him.

For a moment her father looked as though he were about to say something, but he kept silent.

"I don't want Greg anymore, Dad, but I didn't want this to happen. I didn't want him to get hurt or..."

She still couldn't say "die."

"Of course you didn't. No one would."

"You think he was drunk, don't you?" Chelsea asked.

"I don't know, honey. I know Greg likes to drink but anyone can lose control in a blizzard like this."

Chelsea thought of all the swerving cars she and Jansson had passed on their drive to the hospital.

"I'm sure he was drunk. Or high," she whispered.

"What makes you say that?"

"I know him," Chelsea said, "Or rather, I know how he's gotten. He wouldn't care if he wasn't good to drive, the party needed more beer."

"Oh," said Gene.

"I can also feel it in my gut. I'm sure he wasn't sober when he got behind that wheel," Chelsea continued, her heart sinking as she remembered that the story wasn't finished yet.

"What about the other man, the one he hit. What's happened to him?"

Her dad shifted uncomfortably in his chair, as though not sure what to do with his long legs and broad arms in the relatively small seat.

"He's very seriously injured. I believe he's also in surgery now."

"Do we know who he is? Is his family here?" She cast her eye around the waiting room. Apart from the two of them and Vick, there was a waifish looking blonde in her thirties holding a towel tightly around her hand, and a pair of young parents holding their rather red-looking toddler son and looking tense, but no one who looked like Greg's parents; pale and terrified.

"He's not from Foothills, but yes, I know him," Gene said.

"Who is he?"

"It's a long story," Gene said.

"Well, it's going to be a long night," Chelsea said.

Several hours passed. Gene told Chelsea all about the visits he'd gotten from Patrick, the debate with Danielle, Patrick's talk with Mrs. List. He told her how Ron Sciaruto had called him because they couldn't reach Patrick's family and he seemed to be the only person in Foothills who was acquainted with him.

Therese was constantly in and out to go smoke, burned through her whole pack of cigarettes, and then went off to the gift shop to find more. The hospital didn't sell cigarettes, so she gave an orderly who was going off-duty twenty dollars to run across the street to the gas station to buy her another carton. As best as Chelsea could tell, she made a big dent in her next pack between frantic phone calls to Greg's older brother, Michael, and other various family members. Vick didn't move much except to take sips from his soda bottle, and hardly said anything. His eyes darted to the Emergency Room door every time he heard steps but more often than not it was just hospital personnel going about their duties, or a patient being transferred or discharged. After a while, they saw a pair of Foothills police officers leaving the ER. Neither was Ron Sciaruto so Gene didn't dare inquire about Patrick.

"If the cops are here he had to be on something," Chelsea whispered.

She had texted Jansson and told him she would be a while and that her father was with her so he didn't have to wait around for her. He texted back offering to stay, but she urged him to go home and get some sleep. He eventually agreed and told her to let him know if she heard any news.

The snow had finally stopped and the plows were out sanding the roads and pushing all the snow into large heaps by the curbs. The clock seemed to be moving particularly slow. Chelsea steeled herself and finally told Gene who she had been staying with since she left Greg. They were in public; he couldn't get too upset about her staying with a college professor. He took the news considerably well. He asked more about Jansson and Chelsea told him. She didn't go into details about the night she left Greg, however. She knew her dad would be upset by Greg hitting her and now was not the time to bring it up. She would tell him later. At home. Where she would also have to tell him he was pregnant. But that would have to wait. Now was not the time.

It was past four in the morning when someone finally came through the entrance to the ER looking for Greg's parents and brought them back through the big wooden doors.

Chelsea gripped her father's large hand.

"Oh God, this is it," she said.

"What do you mean?" Gene asked.

"I know it. It's bad news. I can feel it."

It was a long time before the Townsends came back out through the Emergency Room door. Vick was supporting Therese who looked as though she were having trouble walking. She was shaking. Both their faces were ashen, shocked. Therese started making small crying sounds. When they reached the area where Gene and Chelsea were,

Chelsea stood up and took a few steps towards them.

Therese buried her face in Vick's shoulder and cried softly.

Vick looked up and Chelsea and their eyes met.

Chelsea's stomach lurched.

Vick slowly shook his head.

25

The sky had grown lighter. The sun was rising. Outside the colors of the dawn reflected majestically on the freshly fallen snow. There were no cars on the road. The morning seemed peaceful; the view outside breathtakingly beautiful. It was taunting her.

Chelsea looked out the window of her dad's truck as they rode back towards Foothills. They would have left the hospital after the Townsends, but wound up having to stay a little longer because Chelsea had thought she might faint when she heard the news about Greg. Her hand flew to her midsection, to her baby, as the room began to sway. One of the nurses rushed out with a wheelchair and ushered them into the hallway in the ER. They took her blood pressure, gave her some orange juice, and let her sit while she steadied herself.

Finally they traipsed out to the pickup and headed back to Foothills. Chelsea had called Jansson to tell him. She said she wanted to stay at his house one last day before going back home with her father. Gene did not question this. He was getting his daughter back; a few more hours didn't matter much.

They drove in silence. When they pulled up to Jansson's house Chelsea turned and hugged her father, hard.

"I love you, Dad." Her voice was squeaking as she tried to hold back her tears.

"I love you, too, Bean."

"I'll call you later tonight. Can you pick me up?"

"Of course I will," Gene said. He watched her climb the farmhouse steps and let herself into Jansson's house with a key. He sat there for a moment, then pulled back out of the driveway and headed for home.

Gene had no sooner collapsed onto his bed when his cell phone rang. He considered silencing it and going to sleep, but thankfully he looked at his caller ID first. It was Ron Sciaruto.

"Hi Gene, it's Ron."

"Ron. You have news for me?"

"We finally got in contact with Frye's family. They are on their way from Utah. They gave me permission to tell you about Patrick."

"What *about* Patrick?" Gene asked urgently.

He had just witnessed a couple facing a parent's worst nightmare. He braced himself for more bad news.

"One of the arteries in his leg was crushed. They had to amputate just below the knee. He also sustained serious head injuries so it's still pretty touch and go. If he pulls through he's looking at a difficult recovery. But he might make it. We just have to wait and see."

Gene let this news sink in.

"Thanks for letting me know, Ron. I really appreciate it."

"You bet," said Ron. "I heard about Greg. I'm sorry."

"I'm sorry, too," Gene said. "I can't imagine what the Townsends are going through."

"There's going to be an investigation."

"I figured," Gene said, thinking of what Chelsea said at the hospital about Greg's drug use.

"Anyway, I've got to go; I just wanted to let you know about the kid."

"Thanks again, Ron."

Gene hung up the phone. Part of his leg amputated and severe head injuries, but Patrick Frye could still come out of this. Gene felt relieved. Insufferable as Patrick's visits had been, Gene felt thankful that Patrick stood a fighting chance. He leaned over and without removing his jacket or climbing under the covers, fell asleep.

Chelsea woke up around two in the afternoon. Jansson made her pancakes, and let her eat them in silence. They spoke a little, and Chelsea was glad to have a few hours with him before she went home. She still hadn't really cried yet. After her initial shock and near-fainting she'd felt mostly numb with disbelief. She wished that her last day with Jansson didn't have to be the same day she found out about Greg. She didn't think she had it in her to lose someone else.

Emboldened by her imminent departure and the reminder that life was so preciously short, Chelsea decided to speak of something she was not ready to hear about until this moment.

"Before I go," she said upon her pancakes, "There's something I want to talk about with you."

"Of course," Jansson said, wondering what could be on Chelsea's mind to discuss following such a traumatic night.

"You remember when you found out about being made department head, so we went out to dinner that night to celebrate?"

Jansson felt as though his blood vessels had turned to ice. He had thought they might never have to talk about that night.

"Yes, I remember," he said cautiously.

Chelsea squirmed in her chair.

"I know we haven't ever mentioned it since, but...I was way more drunk than I let on."

Jansson cocked his head as though he needed to see her more intently.

"I know it. I had more wine than I intended as well."

Chelsea was feeling nauseous now.

"Well, the thing is," she plowed on, goading herself to continue "I remember waking up in your bed half dressed...and...and nothing else. I don't remember what happened that night." She said the last sentence very quickly and felt her face burn with embarrassment. She dropped her gaze and stared at her plate, unable to look at Jansson for the first time ever.

When she didn't hear him respond after several extremely heavy moments, she forced herself to look at him, determined to get an explanation.

Jansson had a curious expression on his face. She couldn't tell whether he was confused or uncomfortable.

"Chelsea," he said finally, his voice breathless and bewildered. "Did you think we slept together that night?"

Completely at a loss, Chelsea mumbled, "I wasn't sure...I couldn't remember...I thought that maybe we might have." She knew her cheeks were bright red now.

"My dear, nothing of the sort happened that night. I would not let it go that far, not with you drunk. I couldn't complicate things even more, not to a young woman whose world was so unsettled."

He was now looking at her in a way she had never seen him gaze at her before. He had in fact looked at her that way many times, but never so she would notice. His eyes were extremely tender, affectionate...even loving.

Chelsea thought back to that night. So there had been no sex. But there hadn't been nothing at all either. Her memory was foggy but she knew it had not been completely innocent.

"But *something* happened that night, I know it, I just can't remember what, exactly."

"I kissed you, Chelsea. That is what happened. I kissed you and you kissed me back for what seemed like ages. And then we fell asleep. I'm sorry I ever let it get that far, it was untoward. I was drinking too, my inhibitions were lowered. It's no excuse, but it ended at kissing."

"You weren't taking advantage of me," Chelsea said quickly, suddenly feeling defensive. "I'm an adult, I wanted it, too." She almost couldn't believe she'd just said that, admitting to feelings for Jansson that she hadn't even admitted to herself.

She was surprised to see him smile.

"I insist on being a gentleman to the end," Jansson declared. "Our friendship was and is more important to me than desires brought on by too much wine. And that friendship, Chelsea, is exactly how it's supposed to be." He reached over and ever so gently brushed a streak of her blonde hair away from her face.

Chelsea called her dad around 8:00 p.m. to come pick her up. She packed all her belongings into her duffel bag, relieved she'd talked everything out with Jansson. They were fine. They were more than fine. At last she knew for sure the baby was Greg's. She would have to sort through everything that came with that later.

She said her goodbyes to Jansson. Knowing she would see him again, and often, she had no regrets about leaving when her father's red pick-up pulled up to the farmhouse.

Gene insisted on meeting Jansson. Chelsea introduced them, worried the exchange might be awkward, but the two men shook hands, exchanged brief pleasantries, and before Chelsea knew it, her dad was carrying her duffel bag out to the truck.

The house was dark when they got home. Gene unlocked the front door and pushed it open. Chelsea knelt down in the doorway and embraced Maudie who bounded up to her and started licking her chin, making excited yelping noises. She couldn't believe she hadn't realized how much she missed her dog.

"You're probably exhausted, you should eat something and then try and get some sleep," Gene said.

"Yes," Chelsea replied, standing back up and walking into the living room, Maudie hot on her heels.

Everything looked the same. Everything smelled the same. She was home. She was safe. But everything still felt broken.

"We can go pick up the rest of your stuff tomorrow afternoon," her dad said. "That is, if you think you can go back to the apartment so soon after..."

"That's fine. I'll be fine. We can go get my things tomorrow, it's not very much." She sat down on the couch. She loved that couch, it was blue and soft and when you sat on it, you sunk into the cushion. It was still dark in the house, only the front hall light was on.

"Chels? How are you doing with all this? I know you and Greg ended on bad terms but you still must—"

"Dad I'm not even thinking about that now," Chelsea said. The truth was she was still numb about Greg. The pain she was feeling now had nothing to do with the accident and went back much farther than the past few days.

There was silence.

"I'm glad you're back, sweetheart" Gene said finally.

"Are you sure you want me back home?" Chelsea's throat was painful trying to subdue a rising sob. The pit of her stomach felt sick, hollow.

Gene stood transfixed.

"How could you even ask that? Of course I want you back home. I've wanted you to come back all along. You belong with your family."

"Yes, and I belonged with my family last year when Mom was dying, too," Chelsea said, her eyes stinging with tears.

Gene made no reply. He knew this, of course, and finally Chelsea knew it as well.

"How can you want me back in the house that I left to be with my shitty boyfriend while my mother was so sick? She was dying; I should have been here every single second and instead I moved out. I walked out on my mom. She needed me and I ruined everything. And all over a guy. " Chelsea's voice was rising and she was really crying now, her words punctuated by sharp gasps and sobs.

Gene remained quiet for a while. He watched his daughter with her head in her hands, shaking as she wept. He had not understood her decision to leave all those months ago. He still did not truly understand it now. But then, there was a lot he did not understand. He did not understand his brother Carl's reaction to his father's stroke. He did not understand his own reaction to the accident, how he felt about what happened to Patrick, and even Greg. But none of that seemed important now. Chelsea was back, and before he could fathom how he was going to forgive her for leaving, he realized that deep down, he already had. Now she had to learn to forgive herself.

"Everyone deals with death and loss differently," he began cautiously. "Maybe you weren't strong enough to see her so sick. Maybe you were too scared to watch her die."

"Oh God, don't sugar coat it, Dad. I was a piece of shit daughter and you know it. I abandoned her and..." Chelsea took several steadying breaths trying to regain control, her voice broke as she said, "God help me, if I could, I would take it all back." Guilt and sadness raged within her, and the violent spasms of her sobbing made her feel sick.

Gene crossed the room and sat beside his trembling daughter on the couch, draping a large arm around her shoulders. She collapsed against him and cried. The two sat in silence for a long time until Chelsea's tears were spent.

"I miss my mother," she whispered weakly.

"I know. I miss her, too," Gene said. "And she knew you loved her Chelsea, even at the very end, she knew you had just lost your way."

Chelsea looked up at him doubtfully. Her head and stomach hurt from the crying and the burning guilt.

"I'm so sorry, Daddy," she said, utterly exhausted both physically and emotionally.

"I know," said Gene. "Believe me. I know. For now, you should get some sleep. We have plenty of time to talk. We have plenty of time to work everything out."

The two of them shared a frozen pizza for dinner as neither of them was very hungry. Afterwards Chelsea dragged herself upstairs to take a hot shower and then fell asleep in her own bed.

Gene, though tired, stayed downstairs. He wanted to see if the stars would be out tonight. It was a crisp, clear night, so he bundled up and went out onto the porch, where he sat and stared up at the sky, although he was absent one dog curled at his feet. Maudie had not left Chelsea's side since she stepped foot back in the house and was now curled up at the end of her bed, as though guarding her.

After a while Gene's exhaustion got the better of him and he returned inside. He put another log into the woodstove, and then headed up the stairs. The sound of his slow, heavy footsteps summoned Maudie out to the hallway. She poked her head out of Chelsea's room as though ready to fight anyone who would take Chelsea away again. Seeing it was just Gene, she relaxed and let him scratch her ears.

"Chelsea's finally home," he told Maudie. "Thank *God*."

"If the stars should appear one night in a thousand years, how would men believe and adore...But every night come out these envoys of beauty, and light the universe with their admonishing smile."

– Ralph Waldo Emerson

Epilogue

Eighteen Months Later...

The seasons were changing again. The incessant rainy days of spring had finally passed, and the crocuses had begun to poke their heads out of the soil weeks ago. Gene stepped out onto his porch and breathed in the delicious smell of the fresh air and basked in the warmth of the afternoon sun. Over a year had gone by since the night of the accident. In some ways both Gene and Chelsea felt that those months seemed to fly by in a heartbeat, and yet at the same time, that night felt like a lifetime ago.

Shortly after Chelsea moved back home she began taking classes at the local community college. She studied biology and now was well on her way to becoming a medical assistant. She also taught a dance class for little girls at her old dance studio twice a week. Of course, she had to cut back on taking classes and teaching to only part-time after her baby was born.

Belinda Rose Shepherd was born July 8 at 10:23 in the morning. She came into the world with giant blue eyes and little blonde peach fuzz on her pink head. Chelsea was secretly thrilled that the baby was a girl, and relieved that she was perfect and healthy. Before long Chelsea started calling her Bell, the name that she would have into adulthood.

Alexander Jansson was a frequent visitor. He regularly joined the Shepherd family for dinner and would often take Chelsea and Bell on outings to the park, and to the aquarium and the zoo. He also often watched Bell when Chelsea needed a night off to catch up on sleep or study for a test. He bought the baby a cozy pink blanket and a large stuffed penguin named Benny who accompanied her everywhere. He loved Chelsea's little girl as though she was his own and for the rest of his life, he never missed a birthday, a school recital, or any other precious milestone that he had painfully missed with his own son. Prompted by Chelsea's reconciliation with her father, Jansson began to make more trips back to Sweden (even taking the Shepherds with him as his guests one summer) to see Gustaf. Although he would never be able to get back all the years he lost with his son, they were slowly able to develop a closer bond that Jansson was committed to keeping.

Although she knew for certain Bell was Greg's daughter, she did not tell Greg's parents about her. She felt conflicted about this, knowing in a perfect world that they should know about their grand-daughter. Even so, she did not want Belinda around the people who had raised Greg, especially given Vick's drinking and Therese's enabling denial.

She did not make this decision lightly. Shortly after Greg's death, she called Greg's brother, Michael, and told him about the pregnancy. Michael lived in California with his wife Audrey, having himself consciously made the decision to distance himself from his parents and their issues. He agreed that the Townsends would be a negative influence on her child, and promised not to divulge any information about Bell to them, but asked if Chelsea would be okay with being in the baby's life himself. Chelsea was happy to oblige, since she had no siblings and it would be good for her child to have an uncle who loved her. Michael and Audrey flew back to Pennsylvania to meet Belinda when she was twelve weeks old. During the visit, Michael informed Chelsea that his parents were moving down to South Carolina in a few weeks and had no plans of ever coming back. Evidently they couldn't deal with their grief in the place they had lost Greg. Chelsea felt this was all for the best.

She felt somewhat guilty that her decision to prevent her daughter from having any kind of relationship with her paternal grandparents. She knew one day Bell would ask about her family and Chelsea would have to justify her reasons for keeping them apart. But she also knew her little girl would start to ask about her father. The day Bell was born Chelsea sat alone and exhausted in the hospital bed after all her visitors were gone, gazing down at her beautiful newborn baby fast asleep on her chest. She was overcome with a myriad of emotions. She felt pure joy at finally meeting her daughter, relief that the labor and delivery was over and the baby was healthy, overwhelming anxiety about how she was going to take care of someone so tiny and helpless, and a nagging sadness that Belinda, the most precious thing to ever belong to Chelsea, also belonged to Greg. She examined the infant from head to toe, trying to see if she could detect any resemblance to Greg Townsend, the person who had once been her whole world. The person whom she had loved, laughed with, lived with before everything had fallen apart.

Her eyes welled up as she thought about how her daughter would not only never know her father, but also that Bell would never know the Greg Chelsea had fallen in love with; the person he had been before the drugs and the fighting; before he had closed himself off to her and struck her in a rage. Tears fell silently down her cheeks as she tried to imagine what in the world she was going to tell Belinda about him, how he used to be, how he'd changed, how he'd hurt her. She knew there would be many conversations over many years about Greg, but it would have to be when Bell was older, when Chelsea was farther away from everything that had happened. In order for her to make sense of Greg's death and her feelings about him, she needed time to heal and she knew deep in her heart that she couldn't do so if Vick and Therese were a part of their world.

Little Belinda was an absolute joy to both Chelsea and Gene's lives. For the first time since before Marybeth passed, their family felt almost whole again, in the process of healing from the raw, fractured state it had been when Chelsea moved out and her mother died.

Yes, the Shepherd family had lost, but it also had reunited and grown. Gene and Chelsea were together again. Motherhood had brought Chelsea a new maturity that made her desperately want to atone for her past self-centeredness, and she was eager to show her father how much she loved and needed him.

Each night after she put Bell down to sleep, she sat and watched her daughter breathe. She felt truly happy, but there was an ache that always gnawed at her, constantly aware of feeling as though she had so terribly failed her own mother, and the sadness she felt knowing Marybeth wasn't there to see her become a mother herself and witness how she'd turned her life around. Chelsea made up her mind to do everything in her power to do right by her daughter.

Gene saw how hard Chelsea was trying and never again mentioned her past choices to leave home. She was home now for the foreseeable future, and all they could do was move forward.

○○

On this particular day, Gene was home from work early and was now sitting with the baby in the rocking chair on the front porch. Gene looked down at his granddaughter, smoothing her light blonde hair. She had beautiful bright eyes, and today she was wearing a pastel pink onesie with little strawberries on it that Tom and Sharon had bought for her. She was an exceptionally smiley baby, quiet, but inquisitive. Sometimes when he watched Chelsea hold her on her lap so that Bell was almost standing, the baby would bounce up and down, as though she was trying to dance. Gene told her this meant they might have another Jumping Bean on their hands. He could see that Chelsea liked the idea that her little girl would one day dance.

Sitting on the porch this early, a long time before the stars were visible, Gene's eyes were not cast upwards towards the sky, but rather upon the remarkable little person who was his granddaughter. She was playing with his car keys and appeared perfectly content to be sitting on his large knee. He listened to her gurgles and watched her shake the keys with her tiny dimpled fist. It was five-thirty in the afternoon and Gene was enjoying the first breath of summer. Holding the baby in one arm, he reached down and pulled a fuzzy yellow stuffed duck out of a bag at his feet and presented it to Bell who began to examine it meticulously.

Maudie lay next to the chair, resting. She was very old and reaching the end of her dog years. It saddened him to think of life in the house without Maudie. The idea of losing such a loyal friend and part of the family only a few years after losing Marybeth made his heart sink. He told Chelsea he planned to start looking for another puppy, mellow like his own Maudie, that he could bring into the house and acquaint with her before she passed. He liked to think that this way the new pup could learn a thing or two about how to behave from a seasoned Shepherd family dog.

He also liked the idea of little Bell being around a dog. Maudie was very good with her. Bell was crawling all over the place and often found herself wherever Maudie happened to be napping. Being a curious infant, she grabbed at the dogs fur, batted her head, and pulled her tail, but Maudie was exceptionally tolerant of the newest little Shepherd.

Gene bounced Bell on his knee absently as he gazed out across the trees. He wondered where Patrick Frye was now and whether the young man had accomplished any part of his mission to save the souls of those who had forgotten Jesus, whether he still had that same unshakeable faith given all that had happened. Gene tried to recollect all the talks he'd had with Patrick, and how the annoying young man handing out Bible verses had impacted his life. Patrick had not convinced Gene to accept Jesus Christ as his personal savior, to attend church, or even to read the pamphlets he had given him. But Patrick Frye had taught Gene something about faith. Not about religion or belief in the divine. Instead he felt he had learned to believe a little bit more in humankind.

Chelsea came out onto the porch.

"Dad, the potatoes and carrots are all peeled and chopped, they're ready to be boiled," she said to Gene.

"Alright," he said shifting to his feet with Bell in his arms, "You take the little one." He gave her to Chelsea, whose arms were outstretched. She took her and kissed her several times on the cheek.

"Hi baby girl," she said moving Bell onto her hip and then swaying her back and forth. Belinda cooed baby noises into Chelsea's shoulder as Chelsea held her and looked out into the afternoon sun.

She thought about how much had changed since her graduation day. How she had changed. How different her life was now. There had been funerals, and births. There had been new friends made, relationships ended, and old ties mended.

And as Chelsea stood there with her little girl, gazing out into the sun, a light breeze brushed by, lifting her hair, filled with the aroma of fast-coming summer. She smiled and for the first time, fully understood why her dad sat on this porch night after night, year after year. The beauty of the perfectly pure blue sky, the warmth of the sunlight on her face, the summer breeze that made the leaves on the trees wave, and finally, the small noises of her baby daughter squirming in her arms, gave Chelsea the same gut feeling Gene Shepherd got from gazing up at the stars. Such a gorgeous afternoon could not happen by accident. It was not meaningless and without purpose. She saw clearly what her dad had talked about all these years and now Chelsea, like Gene, knew there was someone, or something, out there, within her, and all around her, watching over, someone who had given her this beautiful day.

Acknowledgements

There are many people who have provided support and encouragement to me during the writing of *A Wider Universe*. First and foremost I want to express my eternal gratitude to Claudia Gere, without whose enormous wisdom, patient guidance, and expertise, my dream of publishing a novel would never have become a reality.

I am very grateful for the opportunity to have taken two English Lit. courses during my time as an undergraduate at Fairfield University that directly led to the inception of this novel. I want to acknowledge and thank Bob Epstein and Leo F. O'Connor, in whose lectures the inspiration for Gene Shepherd's story was born. The material you assigned and the discussions based upon those works sparked my imagination in ways I could never have expected. I would also like to express my deep appreciation for those who encouraged me to write creatively when there were times I may have been too intimidated to put myself and my work out there; in particular my high school expository writing teacher John Warthen, and my friend

Laura Sabia, both of whom in their own way helped give me the confidence to believe in my own writing.

I wish to extend a big thank you to all the people who have supported me along the way, whether it was through your continued reassurance throughout the writing process, or else your willingness to be beta-readers and offer valuable feedback: Anna Papachristos, the first to say "YES!" when asked to read the earliest draft, Molly Hebert-Wilson, Michelle Oosterman, Frank Fioretti, Tucker Harpin, Ariel Harris, and Herb Scribner. Your support means more than you know. Lastly, I want to thank my mother for her unwavering support, and Anthony, who helps keep me on track and always asks me, "Did you work on your book today?"

Author's Note

Dear Reader,

Thank you for reading *A Wider Universe*. I sincerely hope you have enjoyed reading the novel and getting to know the characters. I also hope that you found the read both interesting as well as thought-provoking.

If you have any questions about Gene, Chelsea, Jansson, or Patrick, I invite you to visit the official *A Wider Universe* Facebook page for further discussion: facebook.com/awideruniversenovel.

I would be happy to respond to your thoughts and comments about the book. You can also follow me on Twitter @AllisonRFloyd or check out my website at www.allison-floyd.com to see what else I am up to these days. I am currently in the process of writing my second novel, so check back for exciting future updates.

Thanks again for reading.

Warmest regards,

Allison Floyd

Made in the USA
Middletown, DE
11 November 2024

64364694R00198